Someone was outside her apartment door.

Liam drew his gun from the concealed holster. He recognized the men outside as part of the gang that had attacked them earlier.

His pulse racing, he turned to Elisabeth.

She gestured with her hand, and they went out the back door. They ran to her car, the intruders gaining on them.

"Come on!" Elisabeth cried, cranking the ignition.

Just then a souped-up SUV pulled into the lot. The driver's voice rose in anger, shouting in a language Liam didn't understand.

But Elisabeth did.

She grabbed Liam's shirt. "Get down! This might be bad."

He hunched down, his eyes only inches from her face. "What do you mean?"

"The men in the SUV... I recognized their tattoos. It's a form of Filipino script popular with gangs."

"Those men in the SUV are gang members..." He blew out a breath as it dawned on him. "There are *two* gangs after us?"

She gave him a wary look. "And we're caught in the middle."

Books by Camy Tang

Love Inspired Suspense

Deadly Intent
Formula for Danger
Stalker in the Shadows
Narrow Escape
Treacherous Intent

CAMY TANG

writes romance with a kick of wasabi. Originally from Hawaii, she worked as a biologist for nine years, but now she writes full-time. She is a staff worker for her San Jose church youth group and leads a worship team for Sunday service. She also runs the Story Sensei fiction critique service, which specializes in book doctoring. On her blog, she gives away Christian novels every Monday and Thursday, and she ponders frivolous things like dumb dogs (namely hers), coffee-geek husbands (no resemblance to her own…), the writing journey, Asiana and anything else that comes to mind. Visit her website, www.camytang.com.

TREACHEROUS INTENT

CAMY TANG

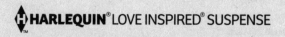

Recycling programs for this product may not exist in your area.

 LOVE INSPIRED BOOKS

ISBN-13: 978-0-373-44641-4

Treacherous Intent

Copyright © 2014 by Camy Tang

www.Harlequin.com

Printed in U.S.A.

So do not fear, for I am with you;
do not be dismayed, for I am your God.
I will strengthen you and help you;
I will uphold you with my righteous right hand.
—*Isaiah* 41:10

For my father-in-law, who fought the good fight,
finished the race and kept the faith.

ONE

Liam O'Neill frowned as he caught sight of the gray Mercedes sedan in his rearview mirror. Hadn't he seen that car behind him several miles back, when he was driving through downtown Sonoma?

He scrubbed his face with one hand as he guided his beat-up pickup truck down the country road. He was exhausted—the nightmares had been especially bad last night. His tiredness was probably making him paranoid. As a skip tracer, tracking down people who didn't want to be found or helping people disappear, he had his share of enemies, but he'd been monitoring the cars behind him and hadn't noticed any obvious tail.

Moments later, the Mercedes turned off onto a side road. Clearly he needed more sleep. He was starting to imagine things.

It had been almost eighteen months since a medical discharge had sent him home from Afghanistan. His shoulder now only had crisscrossing pink scars, but the nightmares and occasional hallucinations hadn't faded as quickly.

His cell phone rang, and he hit the button on his Bluetooth headset to answer it. "Liam."

"It's Shaun."

"Hey, how's Dad?" Liam's brother had taken their father to the hospital that morning.

"Tired. He's home now. But the doctor says he's doing fine. Only a couple more chemo treatments to go. He should be feeling well enough for Christmas in a few weeks."

Liam couldn't share Shaun's optimism. Dad's diagnosis of leukemia a few months ago had rocked him as violently as the mine that had injured his shoulder. The worst part was, cancer wasn't an enemy he could shoot at. He couldn't defend his father the way he defended his unit.

So he did the only thing he could—he tried to burden his family as little as possible while this was going on.

Shaun said, "Monica asked me to call you. Instead of seeing Dad this afternoon, my lovely wife wants to know if you can come tomorrow."

Liam's shoulders tensed. "Is he okay?"

"Yeah. Monica just wants him to nap."

"No problem."

Liam's GPS unit on his dashboard began telling him to turn. "Gotta go," he said to Shaun.

"See you later." His brother hung up just as Liam turned into a long driveway that wound up to a large, rambling farmhouse. The only indications that it was a battered women's shelter were the three security cameras.

He walked up the steps to the front porch and peeked into the window to see what looked like a security room with video monitors, computers and two husky men watching Liam's approach.

There was a security intercom and he pressed the button. "I'm Liam O'Neill, here to see Elisabeth Aday."

"I don't have you on the visitor's list for today, sir," a guard replied.

"I don't have an appointment. I need to ask Ms. Aday a few questions about one of her clients. I don't even need to come inside, if she wants to meet me out here on the porch."

There were heavy footsteps, then the dead bolt drew back and the door opened to reveal a man with a weathered face and jet-black hair. His wary eyes pierced through Liam, but he stepped back to let Liam enter.

He stepped into a short entry hall with a door on either side, one to the security room and another to what looked like a small conference room. The entry hall ended with a stout-looking door, obviously made with reinforced steel. Liam guessed that was the door into the shelter itself.

The security guard said, "I'm afraid I'll have to search you, sir."

Liam submitted readily. He had a permit to carry a concealed weapon, but he'd left his gun locked in his truck. When he had given Liam a pat down and a thorough sweep with a metal-detector wand, the security guard gestured to the conference room. "I'll call Ms. Aday to let her know you're here."

Liam scanned the small room, sparsely decorated with only a large table and chairs surrounding it, and a smaller table in the corner with paper cups and napkins. This must be a place where the women in the shelter could meet with outsiders—close to the security guards and separated from the rest of the house.

Within minutes, he heard the heavy reinforced door open and then close before light footsteps approached. Liam had been expecting the young woman who entered, but he hadn't expected the gut-punch reaction to how beautiful she was.

She wasn't model gorgeous, but there was something about the dark hazel eyes that spoke of courage, pain and compassion. Her skin seemed to glow like gold in the morning sunlight, and her dark straight hair, pulled back into a ponytail, glinted with reddish strands. But her mouth was serious, almost frowning as she looked at him. She studied him for a moment before closing the door and turning to face him.

Her self-composure and the way she waited for him to speak first was what Liam would have expected of a private investigator of her caliber. He found himself wanting to make her trust him as quickly as possible.

"I'm Liam O'Neill."

She nodded but didn't answer.

"I wanted to ask you a few questions about one of your clients."

"I don't speak to anyone about my clients," she said crisply. Her voice was low, husky.

Liam opened his mouth to reply, but he was interrupted by a loud knocking at the front door. They both turned toward the noise, but at the rumbling sound of the security guard's voice, speaking to whoever was outside, Elisabeth turned back to Liam.

"I'm a skip tracer," Liam told her. "A woman named Patricia hired me to find her sister, Joslyn, who disappeared a few weeks ago from San Francisco."

Elisabeth hadn't moved a muscle, but Liam could tell that she had tensed and was trying not to show it.

"Patricia said that Joslyn might be escaping her abusive boyfriend and using a different name," Liam continued. "I found out that a woman named Joslyn came here and that you helped her."

"How do you know it's the same Joslyn?"

"I've been tracking a woman who matches Joslyn Bautista's description." He held up his phone with a photo that Patricia had given to him. "I just want to find out if she's safe. Her sister is worried."

Elisabeth's mouth tightened. Then she said in a strangled voice, "Joslyn doesn't have a sister."

Liam's breath caught in his throat.

At that moment, they could hear a man's voice speaking

loudly through the intercom. "I told you, I'm with Liam O'Neill. I know he's here already." The voice had a faint Filipino accent.

Liam reacted instinctively. He moved toward the conference room door and tried to reach for his concealed gun before remembering he'd left it in the truck. "Get under the table," he ordered Elisabeth before he yanked open the door.

The security guard replied to the man through the intercom, "Sir, Mr. O'Neill is in a conference with Ms. Aday. I'll have to ask him first before I let you inside." The guard turned his head and caught sight of Liam.

"He's not with me," Liam said urgently. "Don't let him—"

There was the deafening blast of a shotgun as the wooden front door exploded into splinters. Liam leaped backward and fell against Elisabeth, who had come up behind him.

The man's voice shouted, "You send Joslyn out here now or we'll blow this place apart!"

Elisabeth stumbled backward into the conference room, landing hard against a chair, as Liam backed into her. The sound of the gunshot still rang in her ears.

She shoved away from Liam. "What did you do? Who are you?"

But Liam's entire body had tensed. There was a haunted look in his dark blue eyes, and though he stared at the open doorway, he didn't seem to see it.

She'd seen behavior like this before in ex-military men. One had reacted in exactly this way to loud *bang* noises— the tensed muscles, the wide unseeing eyes—a waking nightmare brought on by his post-traumatic stress disorder.

Liam carried himself tall and strong, like a soldier, and he wore his hair in a buzz cut that emphasized his sharp cheekbones and wide jaw. Was he ex-military? Was it possible he suffered from PTSD?

He gathered himself together with an effort.

"Liam," she said urgently.

He took a few quick breaths, getting his bearings again, then turned to her. "He's not with me."

"He knew your name."

"He must be working with Patricia—or whatever her name really is." A muscle tightened in his jaw. "You have to believe me."

She had developed a habit of not trusting people readily, but she wanted to believe him. Maybe because his first reaction had been to tell her to get to safety.

Elisabeth moved to the blinds and peeked out. "He's not alone." There was a gray Mercedes parked behind an ancient pickup truck she assumed was Liam's—and three other cars had just pulled up.

The man at the front door looked Filipino, with dusky skin and dark hair, and he waved a shotgun around a bit dramatically. Elisabeth pegged him as a hothead who would shoot first and ask questions later. Behind him, at the base of the porch steps, stood a shorter Filipino man who looked nervous, making Elisabeth wonder if the hothead had been ordered to attack the shelter or if he had done that on his own initiative.

The two security guards had pulled their firearms, but they remained inside the security room. Elisabeth and Liam hovered in the conference room doorway. Her primary weapon was back in the shelter, and she was just about to pull her secondary weapon hidden under her pant leg when the hothead called out, "Where's Joslyn? I want to see her! Or else bring out that Aday woman!"

A shiver spiked through Elisabeth at the mention of her name. Liam shot her a look of concern.

"That's it!" The hothead kicked the door open.

Frank, the security guard closest to the door, jerked back as a piece of wood flew at his face. Bill, the younger guard, recklessly rushed the hothead to try to disarm him.

Liam moved to shield Elisabeth with his body just before the shotgun went off, the sound almost masking Bill's gasp of pain.

Elisabeth peeked out the doorway to see Bill fall to the floor clutching his shoulder, blood seeping between his fingers.

Liam was up from the ground in a flash. Elisabeth followed suit, grabbing her gun from her ankle holster.

Liam elbowed the attacker in the face, making his grip on the shotgun loosen, and then knocked the weapon away. The man threw a punch, but Liam blocked it and grabbed the man in a wrestling move. The two of them spun and staggered in the small entry hallway, thudding against the walls.

The nervous man hesitated at the bottom of the porch stairs. Elisabeth opened the conference room window and fired her pistol into the air. The nervous man ducked and scurried to the open door of the gray Mercedes. "Stay right there," she called out.

Men had emerged from the other three cars, but at her shot, they backed behind their open doors. She wished there was a way for her to help Liam, but the armed men in front had her full attention.

One Filipino man, dressed in an expensive gray suit, purple silk shirt and purple tie, stood up so that he was only partially covered by the door of the car he'd been driving. "We only want Joslyn."

"She's not here. Get in your cars and drive away. No one has to get hurt."

The man's handsome, arrogant face creased in a vicious smile. He obviously wanted to hurt someone—probably Joslyn. Elisabeth hadn't spent much time with the young

woman, but she'd been frightened, penniless and alone
with the distinctive mark of a man's fingers around her
wrist and a strange-looking cut above her eye that Elisabeth guessed was from a ring.

Elisabeth should know. She herself had a strange-
shaped scar above her left cheek.

Had that mark on Joslyn's face been caused by the
flashy gold ring glinting on this man's finger?

"I've already called the police," yelled Frank's voice
from the other window. He must be like her, crouched at
the corner of the open window. Most of the time, Frank
and Bill were needed for enraged ex-boyfriends or husbands who came to demand their women back—not stand-
offs with whole groups of Filipino men in expensive cars
and silk shirts. Elisabeth realized that each of them wore
something purple and gray.

It would take at least fifteen minutes for a policeman to
arrive. Elisabeth hoped they could hold them off for that
long—without anyone getting shot. Liam still struggled
with the other man.

Suddenly, a body flew down the front porch and landed
on the ground. Elisabeth caught a glimpse of dark hair and
a purple sock as a pants leg rode up. It was the hothead.

Immediately, Liam was beside her on the other side of
the window, holding a firearm—probably Bill's. His dark
blue eyes scanned the scene in front, his mouth tight. "How
long before the police can arrive?" he whispered.

"At least fifteen minutes."

"They won't stay put forever."

"We only want Joslyn," the man with the ring repeated
loudly.

"O'Neill was talking to *her*." It was the nervous man,
still huddled behind the Mercedes, speaking to his boss.

Elisabeth tried not to flinch. She had been half hoping
the chaos would make the men forget about what Frank

had told them. They obviously knew all about Liam being hired to find Joslyn.

And now they knew Elisabeth's name. She was on the shelter's website on the volunteer page—her picture, her full name, her website link, for anyone wanting to hire a private investigator who volunteered her services for a battered women's shelter.

Then suddenly Elisabeth heard a faint wailing. A police car, ten minutes sooner than expected. The officer must have already been in the area.

The Filipino men heard it, too. Their leader called, "Let's go," to them in Tagalog, and they got back in their cars. Their driving was impeccably organized—within one minute they were heading down the driveway and turning away from the shelter just as a police car shot into view. It pursued them, red lights flashing.

Elisabeth reholstered her firearm, sagging against the wall next to the window. *This* was something she didn't do every day—have a standoff with eight armed men.

Liam also relaxed, breathing heavily, and lowered his weapon. "Are you all right?"

"I'm fine." Elisabeth studied his tall, muscular frame. He looked like he'd be carrying a few bruises, but thankfully there were no signs of blood.

He turned the full force of those dark blue eyes on her, and she found it hard to breathe. She hadn't been attracted to any man in so long…ever since Cruise. The name of her ex-boyfriend was like a bucket of cold water, and Liam turned back into just a man—a handsome one, but not one to be trusted.

"I'm sorry." Liam's voice was hoarse.

"For almost getting me shot or for ruining my morning?" she quipped. She needed to get some distance from what had just happened. And from the emotional intensity in Liam's eyes.

"Those men must have followed me. While I was driving, I thought I might have been tailed, but I wasn't sure."

"They had four cars here. They might have used a four-car team to tail you, which would have been harder to notice."

Unease crept into his eyes. "But what's worse is that they followed me straight to *you*."

TWO

He'd just put an innocent woman in danger.

No, it was even worse than that. He'd put *two* innocent women in danger.

The fact that Liam had practically delivered Elisabeth to those men on a silver platter filled him with guilt as police officers swarmed around the women's shelter. Some of the residents were outside now, looking fearfully at the broken front door, while police officers ranged around the property, going in and out of the house through side doors.

An ambulance had pulled up front and the injured security guard, Bill, was being patched up from where his shoulder had been grazed. The older security guard was giving Bill an earful about his foolhardy actions.

Detective Carter of the Sonoma Police Department had just arrived. Liam had worked with the man several times over the past few months, contracted by the Sonoma police to track people down.

"Did you catch any of the men who drove away?" he asked Detective Carter as the officer approached.

He shook his head, his thinning red-gold hair glinting in the sunlight. "Officer Fong happened to be nearby when the security guards hit their direct signal to dispatch, but the four cars split up as soon as they left the driveway. Officer Fong followed one of them but lost the car."

Elisabeth sighed. "I guess it was too much to hope that we got a couple of them for questioning."

"You don't know who they were?" Detective Carter asked.

She shook her head. "I think they were Filipino. The leader spoke in Tagalog to his men."

"What exactly did they want?" Detective Carter asked.

"They demanded that we turn over one of my clients," Elisabeth said.

"What client?"

"She told me her name was Joslyn Flores."

"A few days ago, a woman who called herself Patricia hired me to find her sister, Joslyn Bautista," Liam said. "She'd disappeared a few weeks ago, and her 'sister' was worried."

"Nothing about it seemed unusual?" Detective Carter asked.

Liam grimaced. The detective had often praised Liam's gut instincts, but they seemed to have failed him this time. "She seemed sincere. It was a little unusual when she paid the deposit in cash, but she said it was because she didn't want her husband to know because he didn't believe Joslyn was missing. I ran a cursory background check on her and she seemed to be who she said she was. The records showed that Patricia's last name had been Bautista before she'd married Henry Santos, and her sister, Joslyn, lived with them in Los Angeles."

"I know Joslyn didn't have any sisters," Elisabeth said. "When I was training her to go off grid, she had to be honest with me about any relatives she might run into. I saw her face. She wasn't lying to me when she said she didn't have siblings."

"I should have dug deeper. A hacker could have created a credible background for Patricia," Liam said. "Patricia said that Joslyn may have been traveling under a different last name. I followed a few leads that pointed to Ms. Aday." Liam nodded to Elisabeth. "That's why I came here today, to ask her if she'd helped Joslyn."

"Did you tell Patricia you were coming here today?" Detective Carter asked.

"No. When I was driving here, I thought I might have been tailed but I couldn't be sure. The men came in four cars, so they might have traded off tailing me."

"Hiring a hacker and using a four-car tail?" Detective Carter frowned. "This isn't some small operation. These guys are organized and have money."

Liam told him about speaking to Elisabeth and being interrupted by the man at the front door who claimed he was with Liam. "The guard let slip that I was with Elisabeth. He mentioned her by name." If only he'd been a second faster, he could have prevented that guard from saying anything.

Detective Carter looked sharply at them both. "So if he didn't know who you'd come to see, he does now."

Liam explained about the man shooting the door and rushing in, about Bill jumping him and Liam struggling with him. It had been a lot harder than he'd expected because his injured shoulder had flared up. He rubbed it, still feeling the ache.

Detective Carter noticed. "Your shoulder still okay?"

"It's fine."

The detective shook his head. "I want you to see the paramedic when we're done here."

"Detective—"

"Injuries like that are always bad." The detective's gray eyes on Liam were steely but concerned. "You don't want to learn you've made things worse when you're in the middle of chasing someone and you find you can't pull yourself over a fence."

Liam put his hands up in mock surrender. "Fine."

"What injury?" Elisabeth asked.

"Shoulder wound. Afghanistan," Liam said. It was bad enough his injury had worried his dad. Now even Detective Carter was interrupting taking their statements to worry about him. Liam couldn't have that.

Elisabeth studied his face for a moment, and surprisingly she seemed to understand his reluctance to draw attention to his shoulder. She turned back to Detective Carter. "I tried to see the license plate but didn't have a good enough angle."

"I only saw a partial as they got away," Liam said. "Three-T-something."

Detective Carter noted it down in his notebook.

She explained the rest of what happened. Liam winced again when she mentioned how the man had told his boss that she was talking to Liam.

Detective Carter's expression was alert. "They only got your last name?"

"But I'm on the shelter website. Full name, photograph and my professional contact info. The men only needed to use a smartphone to check the website to find me."

"And you have no idea who they were and why they wanted Joslyn?" Detective Carter asked.

"Four cars seems excessive for an angry ex-boyfriend who wants her back," Liam said.

"She never mentioned anything about her ex," Elisabeth said. "She was scared and penniless. Luckily she didn't need medical attention when she arrived. She left as soon as she could."

"That seems unusual," the detective said.

"It is. Most women are relieved to find somewhere safe. They're not yet thinking about the future. Joslyn was grateful to the shelter, but she was still anxious to move on. She took off early one morning and no one saw her leave."

"Ms. Aday, you're in danger if they think you know where Joslyn is," Detective Carter said.

"They don't know for sure that she's not at the shelter," Elisabeth pointed out.

"I don't know how long that'll keep them from trying to find you," Liam said. He saw the shiver that passed over her.

"I'll post an officer here to make sure the shelter's safe from any other attacks," the detective said. "But I'm afraid we're stretched pretty thin. Unless you're directly threatened, I don't believe I can get authorization for a protective detail on either of you."

Elisabeth said, "Don't worry, I can take care of myself," at the same time that Liam said, "I'll be fine."

"I know you're both pretty competent, but just be careful." He nodded to them and went to talk to one of the other officers nearby.

"You need some type of protection," Liam blurted out. "Let me help you. It's my fault they're after you now. I led them here."

She blinked in surprise, and he thought he saw a hint of warmth in her hazel eyes at his concern for her. But then she lifted her chin. "I'm a licensed private investigator with advanced tactical and defensive handgun training. I think I'll be okay."

He was impressed. Still… "No one can be completely safe on their own. Personally, I know I wouldn't stand a chance against eight men. The two of us could help each other out."

Again, she blinked at him. Now she looked wary. "Help each other to do what?"

"Figure out who those men are, and why they want Joslyn so badly." Liam looked deep into her eyes, wanting her to understand how sincere he was. "Let me help you."

* * *

Those dark blue eyes were almost hypnotic.

Elisabeth couldn't look away from Liam. Finally, she had to close her eyes and turn her head away.

He wanted to protect her. It had been so long, she'd forgotten what it was like to rely on someone else, to not have to always stand on her own two feet.

But trusting someone wasn't who she was anymore. She'd had to learn that lesson the hard way—she wasn't about to open herself up to that again.

Still, she had to admit she was touched by the deferential way he spoke to her, as if he really respected her abilities and wasn't just placating her. Most of the men she encountered—the ones who had betrayed her and the abusers who came to the shelter in search of their victims— were condescending in the way they treated women. It surprised her to find one who wasn't.

And really, who was she kidding? What chance did she have against eight armed men? She might be stubborn, but she wasn't stupid.

She kept her expression cool, calculating. "What did you have in mind? I'm not much into someone shadowing my every step."

He smiled and it transformed him, softened his wide jaw, making his eyes gleam. "I promise I'm house-trained."

"Good, because I just got a new apartment here in Sonoma." A muscle in her neck spasmed. She hadn't meant to share that. There was something about Liam, some aura of safety he emitted that enveloped her, too, and made her let down her guard. She couldn't afford to do that.

Liam looked at the people milling around, and with a gentle hand on her elbow, guided her down the long driveway.

"For starters, let's see if we can reconstruct what happened with Joslyn. How did she find the shelter?"

"I have a few contacts in Los Angeles, some churches and shelters. They refer women to this shelter if they have an especially vindictive or persistent abuser."

"You have no idea where Joslyn might have gone from here?"

Elisabeth chewed her lip. Was Liam truly trustworthy? But she trusted Detective Carter—she'd seen him handle some of the men who had found their victims at the shelter, and the other volunteers had always spoken highly of him. From his manner with Liam, Detective Carter obviously had respect for him. "I'm not sure," Elisabeth said slowly, "but when I was coaching her, I mentioned Oregon once as an option, and she seemed interested."

"Oregon's a big state."

"I also taught her how to hide, and it might not be safe for us to even try to find her. I don't want to lead these men straight to her. If it comes down to it, I won't risk Joslyn's safety. I'd rather work on this end and try to find out who they are and why they're after her."

"Joslyn didn't say anything about who she was running from?"

"No." Elisabeth thought back to her short few days with Joslyn. "She had been badly beaten about a week before. She had bruises fading from her arms and shoulders, a cut on her face, a broken rib—I think she'd been kicked—and a broken hand. Her injuries had all been bandaged up by some clinic or emergency room."

Liam's expression had become grave and hard as she listed Joslyn's injuries. "Her ex-boyfriend did that to her?"

"She seemed afraid of him, but at the same time, I thought there was some anger behind all that fear, which is unusual." She then remembered something. "She might have had ligature marks on her wrists. At least, they looked that way to me, and they were her freshest bruises."

"He *tied* her?" His voice was muffled by his tight jaw.

Men's anger used to make Elisabeth flinch. As she'd regained her self-esteem, she'd had to train herself to face it with calm confidence, remembering she was no longer that victim. But Liam's anger, directed at the man who'd hurt Joslyn, made Elisabeth realize he was someone who wouldn't stand for anyone lifting a finger to her. What would it be like to have someone who wanted to guard her and care for her? She hadn't had anyone like that since she was sixteen, when her mother died.

"Some abusers do that, but it's unusual," she said.

"The way I see it, the only way you or I will ever be safe is to figure out what's going on," Liam said.

"It sounds better than just sitting around and waiting," she admitted. "Let's talk to some of the women at the shelter to see if anyone knows anything about Joslyn."

Liam nodded, but as they walked back up the driveway toward the house, he said, "We'd better be discreet. Detective Carter might not appreciate us doing our own investigation when the police are on it already."

"I'm a private investigator. This is my job." They walked in silence for a few moments, then she said, "You're pretty friendly with Detective Carter."

"He's known my family for a long time. When I started my skip-tracing business, he sent some work my way."

"I do some freelance for the San Francisco FBI," she found herself saying, and bit her lip to keep herself from blurting out more. What was it about Liam that made her so eager to overshare about her life? "Sorry, I didn't mean to sound like I was bragging."

His eyes twinkled at her. "An occasional dose of humility is good for a man's character."

She didn't know what to say. She hadn't often met men who could make fun of themselves this way.

At the back of the house, there was a fenced-in recreation area for the residents, and Elisabeth knew the key combination to open the gate. She nodded to Witton—one of the house security guards—who stood watching over the children on the play set. As soon as some of the women saw her, they came up to talk.

"Are you all right?" Kalea, a staff member at the house, grasped Elisabeth's hand, but she also cast a curious look at Liam.

"I'm fine. This is Liam O'Neill. He's a skip tracer and he works with Detective Carter."

Several of the women visibly relaxed.

Elisabeth gave an abbreviated account of what had happened.

"Joslyn?" Kalea's eyebrows rose. "But she left weeks ago."

"Do those men still think she's here?" Witton's dark brows lowered over his deep-set eyes.

"Not sure," Liam said. "Detective Carter is assigning some officers to watch over the house, though."

"What do they want with her?" Kalea asked.

"We don't know," Elisabeth said.

Kalea looked thoughtful. "She didn't say much when she was here."

"She enjoyed playing with the children," one of the women spoke up.

"Miss Joslyn was sick," said Kayoi, a precocious little girl with large eyes and a narrow chin.

Her mother tried to hush her, but Elisabeth said, "No, I'd like to know what Kayoi saw." She knelt in front of the girl. "What do you mean, she was sick?" From what Elisabeth could tell, Joslyn had been healthy, aside from her injuries.

"She was throwing up in the bathroom," Kayoi said. "Early in the morning, before breakfast."

Joslyn could have been vomiting for a variety of reasons, but one zoomed to the top of Elisabeth's list.

"I asked her if she wanted me to get Miss Kalea, but Miss Joslyn said she was only a little sick and didn't need help."

"Thank you, Kayoi. That's helpful." Elisabeth rose to her feet and caught Liam's eye. From his expression, she figured he had made the same guess.

"Was she pregnant?" Kalea asked in a low voice.

"If she was, she didn't tell me," Elisabeth said.

Kalea leaned close to her. "Are you in danger from those men who are after her? Are you going to be all right?"

Elisabeth didn't want to lie to her, but she didn't want to worry her, either. However, Liam answered for her. "I'll keep her safe. Don't worry."

His words should have annoyed her—after all, she was able to take care of herself. But his tone was earnest rather than arrogant, and if she was honest with herself, it was good to know someone had her back.

Not that she'd let herself rely on that. No, he might sound trustworthy now, but she'd seen too many broken promises to start trusting someone now just because they seemed earnest. He wanted to protect her? Fine. But she wouldn't stop protecting herself.

Kalea squeezed Elisabeth's hand. "We'll be praying for you, okay?"

Elisabeth's answering smile was stiff. She loved volunteering at Wings shelter, but the faith of the owners and the staff occasionally made her uncomfortable. She didn't feel any affinity to a God who had failed her at some key points in her life.

She spoke to a few of the other women there, giving reassurances and answering questions, but she learned nothing new about Joslyn. She had just left a group of women when she saw Tiffany sitting alone on a bench, soaking in the sun. Tiffany didn't obviously signal to Elisabeth, but she held her gaze and tilted her head slightly. Her expression was anxious.

Elisabeth casually walked over and sat beside her. "How are you feeling?"

Tiffany rubbed a hand over her distended stomach. "Tired. The baby's been kicking a lot lately."

"So you heard that the men were looking for Joslyn?"

Tiffany nodded. She whispered, "I saw her, the night she left."

"What happened?"

"I woke up in the middle of the night to go to the bathroom. When I was heading back to bed, I spotted Joslyn just as she was closing her door. She looked scared to see me. I knew right away she was leaving. I tried to get her to stay, I told her she was safe here."

"She didn't believe you?"

"Joslyn said that he'd never stop looking for her until she was dead, because she'd embarrassed him. She said that she had seen him kill a man for no good reason, so he'd certainly kill her."

Elisabeth started in surprise. "She witnessed a murder?"

"I told her to speak to Detective Carter, but she said she didn't have proof outside of what she saw, and she wouldn't live to testify against him. She was certain that the only way she'd ever be safe would be when he was in jail, and until then, she had to keep running from him. And then she left." Tiffany's lips were white. "Was he the man who came to the shelter today?"

"I don't know." She took Tiffany's hand. "But don't worry. You're safe here."

Tiffany nodded, but her shoulders still hunched, as if trying to protect her unborn child. "Please don't tell anyone I told you about this."

"I won't." Elisabeth gave her hand a final squeeze, then went to speak to some other staff workers.

She was distracted by the sound of children squealing. Liam had entered into a tickle war with four children at once, and they were having a grand time. Liam squirmed out of the way of little hands even as he wiggled his fingers at tummies, making the children shriek and leap aside.

The mothers laughed, and the joyful sounds seemed to erase the somber mood. The women came here out of such pain, and this lighthearted play seemed to Elisabeth to bring not just a respite but also a sense of hope for the future. And it was all because of Liam.

Finally, Elisabeth and Liam decided to leave. Two little boys clung to his legs and rode along for a few steps as he walked.

"Please, Mr. Liam, don't go," one of them said, looking up at him.

"You can stay in my bed," the other one said.

Liam grinned and managed to untangle their little arms from his legs, ruffling their hair. "I'll come back."

As they left, Elisabeth said, "You're really good with kids."

"I like them." The grin was still on his face. "I hope I have—" He stopped abruptly, and his smile faded.

Did he hope to have kids of his own? Why would that thought make him so sad?

You're being nosy, Elisabeth told herself. Never mind that she was an investigator and she was always observing people. She didn't want to wonder about Liam or his life. She wasn't even sure it was a good idea to partner with him. She just wasn't used to working with someone. She usually only depended on herself, and that was what she was comfortable with.

That thought suddenly made her feel very alone.

She shook it off and refocused on Liam. "If Joslyn is pregnant, that might be what had spurred her to run away. She'd want to protect her baby."

Elisabeth also told Liam what Tiffany had said— keeping Tiffany's name out of it, as she'd requested—about Joslyn witnessing her ex-boyfriend murdering someone.

"We need to look into that murder," Liam said. "Joslyn said she had no evidence, but with our skills and training, we might find something she missed. And to start, we could look into the men who attacked us today."

"Did you notice their clothes? They all wore purple and gray. Was it a uniform? Are they part of some organization?"

Liam hesitated, then said, "Gang colors."

Elisabeth thought about it. "Maybe. There are a lot of Filipino gangs up and down the West Coast. But they're mostly in the big cities."

"They could be from one of the cities. That murder Joslyn witnessed might be important enough to make them drive to Sonoma." Liam looked thoughtful. "I have a friend who used to be LAPD. He could chat with someone from the gang task force. But that's just for Los Angeles."

"I'll call some of my contacts with the San Francisco FBI."

"Maybe Detective Carter has contacts in Portland and Seattle."

"We have to find a way to put Joslyn's ex-boyfriend in jail, just like Joslyn said," Elisabeth said. "Until then, none of us will be safe."

THREE

"The Bagsic gang?" Elisabeth paused in the act of unlocking her apartment door. Next door, her neighbor's dog barked frantically at them from behind the closed front door.

Liam nodded as he tucked his cell phone back in his pocket. "Nathan didn't even have to ask his friends in the LAPD. He recognized the colors right away."

"So he's encountered the gang before?" Elisabeth let them inside, pausing to deactivate the security alarm. The dog's barking leveled off as they went inside.

Liam's first impression of her apartment was cream and sand, neutral colors, but rather than being soft or soothing, the decor felt almost sterile. Her furniture was all modular and new, although inexpensive, and everything was clean lines, simple design. Even the Christmas wreath on the front door had only simple gold balls decorating it. There were no other Christmas decorations. It struck Liam as being a sort of fortress rather than a home.

Elisabeth turned to look at him, and he realized she was waiting for an answer.

"Nathan used to be in the narcotics unit. He sometimes had to deal with the Bagsics, although they weren't as active in his district. They deal in crystal meth."

Elisabeth nodded and headed to the kitchen. "Want anything to drink? Water?"

"Yeah, thanks."

He'd jumped at her suggestion that they go to her apartment to do their research, partly because the internet connection at his place wasn't always reliable, and partly because he was reluctant to bring her to the shabby duplex he rented on the outskirts of town. Focused on building his skip-tracing business, utilizing the computer skills he'd learned in the military, he hadn't bothered with furnishings even in the eighteen months he'd been home. So he had one small card table to hold his computer and exactly three chairs. He had no curtains at the front window and he still didn't even have a bed frame for his mattress. His sister-in-law Monica had just forced a garage-sale couch on him.

But from the day he'd moved in, he'd had pictures of his family and friends on the windowsill. He displayed his signed Buster Posey baseball and other mementos, like a slightly misshapen pottery bowl that his deceased sister had made for him when she was in high school. It held some Celtic coins and a claddagh ring that had belonged to his mother. He also displayed his vintage watch collection—nothing too expensive, but special to him because they had belonged to family members—and a few paperback books.

In contrast, Elisabeth's apartment had no personal touches. No pictures on the narrow white mantel above the living room's small fireplace, no mementos on the side table. There were the framed diplomas on the wall for her college degrees in psychology and criminal justice, and the multiple computer monitors set up on a table in a tiny dining room.

He realized that the apartment wasn't a fortress—*she* was. What had happened to her that made her wall herself off?

She entered the dining room with glasses of water for them both and nodded toward the computer paraphernalia. "Pull up a chair."

Liam had brought in his laptop with him in a case, so he found a clear space on the table and booted it up. Elisabeth gave him the password to her wireless internet network— or rather, one of her wireless internet networks. She had several, some with high-security protection. He also noticed that her desktop computer, which rested underneath the table, was hardwired into the cable internet and had a secondary security box attached.

He must have looked surprised, because she noticed his face and said, "I have to be careful because I have information on women on the run from some really bad men. It's truly a matter of life and death if one of the abusers manages to find his victim."

Liam also suspected she had a high security clearance for the work she did for the FBI. The security measures were likely for that information, too.

"So here's what we have," he said as she fired up her computer. "Joslyn is somehow connected to the Filipino Bagsic gang from Los Angeles. My guess is her ex-boyfriend is a gang member."

"It makes sense. They have the money to hire someone like Patricia and to pay a hacker to make sure a background check raised no flags. The gang is probably involved in whatever murder Joslyn witnessed. We need to figure out what murder it was."

"If Joslyn witnessed it, the victim might be someone who was connected to her. But to find out who it was, we need Joslyn's real name. I doubt it was the one Patricia gave to me."

"We need her boyfriend's name, too."

The worked side by side for an hour. Liam was used to working in silence by himself, but he found, to his surprise, that it was helpful to have someone there to bounce ideas off, or to have them offer tidbits of info they discovered in their searches. However, they couldn't find Joslyn's real last name, nor her boyfriend.

Liam heaved a sigh. "The problem is that the Bagsic gang members use nicknames, not their real names, on social media."

"Or just their first names. And they're careful about not declaring their gang affiliation on the internet." Elisabeth frowned at her computer screen. "I wish we had more on Joslyn herself."

They were interrupted by the sound of Elisabeth's neighbor's dog barking frantically, followed by the doorbell.

Elisabeth tensed. "I'm probably just being paranoid. I get visitors often enough." She looked through the peephole, and her shoulders immediately relaxed. "It's Kalea, from the women's shelter."

She opened the door. "Come on in."

"No, I just stopped by to give you this." Kalea handed her a crayon drawing on a piece of paper. "Kayoi drew this for you and insisted I give it to you today." Kalea rolled her eyes.

Elisabeth smiled. "Tell her thanks."

"See you!" Kalea waved and left.

Elisabeth shut the door and returned to the dining room. Her eyes softened as she looked down at the drawing. "This is the third drawing this month that she's done for me."

"Could I see it?"

She handed it to Liam. It was a very colorful picture with people scattered around a green field, with a jungle gym drawn in the corner. There were several children, each portrayed a little differently, and four adults—one with an *S* on her shirt, one with a ponytail, one with curly brown hair and one with long dark hair.

As Elisabeth pointed toward the people on the page, her neighbor's dog started barking frantically again.

"The ponytail is probably me," Elisabeth said. "The long dark hair is her mother. The curly hair is either Kalea or Tiffany, and the *S* on her shirt…" Elisabeth's brow wrinkled. "Wait a minute…"

The dog was still barking. It had only barked like this when Liam and Elisabeth, and then Kalea, had been outside her apartment door. But Kalea was gone.

Someone else was outside her apartment door.

Liam shot to his feet. "No one knocked, right?"

"It might just be one of the neighbors walking past."

"No harm in checking." He drew his gun from the concealed belt holster he'd put back on after leaving the shelter.

He checked the peephole but saw no one in front of her door. Liam stepped behind a curtain to the side of the front window and barely touched the blinds to peek outside.

Two Filipino men in purple and gray stood outside Elisabeth's front door, angled to avoid appearing in her peephole. Neither of them was the leader from today's attack, but Liam remembered seeing one of them coming out of one of the other cars—he had a pockmarked face, puffy cheeks and a slightly bulging belly over his dark gray jeans.

Liam's pulse raced, and he turned to silently signal Elisabeth to remain quiet. She nodded from her position a few feet away, slowly pulling a gun out of her purse. Her slim body was taut, alert. Although they both had their weapons, he would do everything in his power to avoid using them. This was a residential area, with families and children. A stray bullet could seriously injure or even kill someone.

He looked out again. The two men were talking in low

voices, so low that he only heard a barely audible rumble. He probably wouldn't have understood them anyway if they were speaking in Tagalog. What were they intending to do? Break down the door? Pick the lock?

One of the men moved to the front window to try to peer inside, and Liam moved against the wall so he couldn't be seen. Elisabeth also ducked out of sight.

When the man's shadow moved away from the blinds, Liam peeked outside again. One man crouched near the front doorknob with lock-picking tools, working frantically, while the other stood guard. Liam guessed that the neighbor's dog barking spurred them to get inside before drawing more attention to themselves.

Liam mouthed to Elisabeth, "Is there a back door?"

She nodded and gestured with her head toward the kitchen. She only paused to reach under the table to grab a laptop case before she led the way. Liam also stopped to grab his laptop. In the kitchen, he whispered, "What about your desktop computer?"

"It's password protected and the data is backed up on a secure cloud server," she said. "If they try to hack my hard drive, it'll go into security lockdown mode and wipe itself clean."

The back door led from the kitchen out into a minuscule patio, which in turn led to a paved path that wound past the apartment complex. Elisabeth checked outside to make sure the two men hadn't sent someone to watch the back, but there was no one there.

"Where does this path lead?" Liam asked while holstering his gun and settling his laptop in its case.

"To the south exit of the complex, or the front of this row of apartments."

"They'll see us if we try to run for our cars."

"If we wait a bit, they'll be inside my apartment, and we can go for it."

"Let's take your car," Liam said quickly. His beat-up pickup was not going to cut it if the two men gave chase. Elisabeth's Chevy sedan was in much better shape.

But they waited a second too long. When they darted for the parking lot, they heard Elisabeth's back door open and a man's shout. Elisabeth already had her car key in her fingers by the time they reached the car. Liam waited next to the passenger door, his leg twitching as he watched the man run closer to them.

"My next car is going to have remote unlock," she muttered as she yanked her door open. She dived into the car and reached over to unlock the passenger door, and Liam climbed in.

The two men bore down on the car that sputtered as the engine tried to turn over. "Come on!" Elisabeth cranked the key in the ignition.

At that moment, a car pulled into the parking lot, a souped-up SUV gleaming with chrome, with elaborate scrollwork detail all along the side. The two men barely glanced at the SUV, even when the driver of the car, a man, shouted to them.

But then the driver's voice rose in anger and spat out a sentence in a language Liam didn't understand.

Elisabeth froze, checking over her shoulder at the newcomers.

A passenger stuck his head out the window to yell at the two men, also. He sounded even angrier than the driver.

"Oh, no," Elisabeth breathed. She grabbed at Liam's shirt. "Get down!"

He folded in half, his eyes only inches from Elisabeth's face.

Men's voices rose even louder. It sounded like there were at least three men in the SUV, and the two Bagsic gang members who had been chasing them were yelling, too. Then the SUV's engine roared, and the squealing of tires shrieked in Liam's ears. There were two shouts of surprise.

Elisabeth and Liam raised their heads up to peek out. The two Bagsics were cutting across the lawn between two apartment buildings and running toward the street. The SUV tried to chase them but couldn't fit in the grassy alleyway, and so it raced out of the small parking lot.

Elisabeth didn't wait. She started the engine and cleared the parking lot, headed in the opposite direction from the other men and the SUV.

"What happened?" Liam asked.

Elisabeth didn't answer right away. She seemed to be thinking hard. When she stopped at a stoplight, she finally said, "This might be bad."

"What do you mean? What did the men in the SUV say? They were Filipino, right?"

She nodded. "They said, 'What are you doing here, Bagsic scum?'"

"The men knew they were Bagsic gang members?" Liam ran through the list of who would be familiar with the gang colors. Law enforcement. People who lived in the area the Bagsics ruled. Drug addicts who bought the Bagsics' crystal meth. And... He grew cold. "Who were those men?"

Elisabeth chewed roughly on her lower lip, something Liam noticed she did when she was stressed.

"I couldn't say for sure, but—the Bagsics yelled back something like, 'You've got some nerve, Toomies.' I think that's what they said. And then they started insulting their parentage."

"Toomies? Who are they?"

"I don't know, but did you notice anything about the hands on the men in the SUV?"

"They both had wide tattoos around their wrists. The tattoos looked similar."

"I think they were. I only got a glimpse of the design, but I think the tattoos were Baybayin."

"What?"

"It's a form of ancient Filipino script. It's gotten popular for tattoos."

"And both those men had the same design." Liam blew out a deep breath. Rather than colors—or perhaps in addition to colors—they had tattoos. "Those men in the SUV were gang members. Some rivals to the Bagsics."

The light turned green and Elisabeth drove on. She gave Liam a wary look. "But why are they in Sonoma?"

FOUR

"All my efforts to keep my home address private, and the gang found my apartment within a few hours." Elisabeth told herself to breathe deeply, but the frustration and anger made her breaths short and harsh.

Liam kept looking behind them to make sure they weren't followed. "They probably followed Kalea from the shelter."

She knew that, but hearing him say it made a chill pass over her. Would Kalea be all right?

Liam continued, "If she hadn't come here on her way home, they might have followed her home and then attacked her to make her tell them where you live." He rubbed his hand over his face. "I'm just grateful to God that she stopped by your apartment."

What did God have to do with it? Elisabeth almost asked out loud, but stopped herself. She was being overly emotional after what had happened. "We need to call Detective Carter. Maybe he can send a patrol car to watch over Kalea's house."

"We need to call him about the attack anyway." He took out his cell phone.

While Liam explained to Detective Carter what had happened, Elisabeth concentrated on calming down so she could think clearly. Long-term planning didn't come automatically to her, but she'd worked hard to learn to stop and think ahead. She took in one breath through her nose, then another.

The gang was clearly prepared to target Elisabeth in order to find Joslyn. In order to get the Bagsics off her back, she still needed to find out more about Joslyn, her ex-boyfriend and the murder she'd witnessed. She and Liam needed an internet connection and a safe place to do their work. But where? She didn't want to put anyone in danger.

Liam got off the phone. "Detective Carter said he'll send someone to Kalea's house. He's also sending someone to your apartment right away. I told him we'd meet the officer there."

Elisabeth nodded and turned the car around.

The apartment doors were still unlocked, but otherwise it looked the same as when they'd left. Officer Joseph Fong arrived quickly. He was the same policeman who had arrived first at the women's shelter this morning, and who had given chase to the escaping gang members.

"Hey, Liam, twice in one day," the young policeman joked. "I'm going to think you're my fans."

"Or you're ours," Liam said with a smile.

Officer Fong cleared Elisabeth's apartment for them, but it was empty, as they had expected. He took their statements.

"At least they didn't do any damage to the place," the officer said. "From what you said, it sounds like they left to chase after you two practically as soon as they broke in."

"There were other guys who showed up," Liam said, and told him about the souped-up SUV who chased after the gang members. Liam and Elisabeth both tried to draw the scrollwork they'd seen on the side of the SUV, but both their efforts were pretty bad.

"Were any of those the same guys from this morning?" Officer Fong asked.

Liam told him about the pockmarked man he'd recognized, and confirmed that both the men who had broken in were dressed in purple and gray.

"If I'd known this morning they were Bagsics, I'd have used a different tactic when trying to drive after them." Officer Fong gave a huff of frustration. "Bagsics are known for their driving skills."

"That's right, you were in LAPD before you came to Sonoma," Liam said.

The officer nodded. "When I heard your statement about what the men were wearing, I recognized the gang colors right away and told Detective Carter."

"What else can you tell us about the Bagsics?"

"They're not a huge gang, and they're better organized than most," Officer Fong said. "The leadership is smart, but the younger captains are more impulsive, and it causes friction. At least, that's what the situation was when I was down in L.A."

"They're into meth dealing?" Liam asked.

"Big-time. The LAPD has been trying to crack down on the Bagsics' ephedrine supply—the precursor for meth production—from the Philippines, but they haven't been able to stop their shipments into the Port of Los Angeles. Because it's the Bagsics, we should have a patrol car check up on you—"

"I'm not staying here," Elisabeth said. "I'll find somewhere to lie low."

Officer Fong looked uncertain about her answer, but then his police radio crackled. "All right. I'll get going. Let us know if you need anything." With a wave, the policeman headed back to his squad car and drove off.

"I feel exposed," Elisabeth said as she and Liam went back inside her apartment. "I don't want to stay here now that the gang knows where I live. What if they show up with guns blazing and one of my neighbors gets injured by a stray bullet?"

Liam nodded. "I've been thinking about that. My friend Nathan just bought a house on the outskirts of Sonoma. If we take the time to make sure we're not followed, we can stay there for a little while and the gang won't find us."

Liam explained that Nathan was ex-LAPD and now worked as head of security for a high-end apartment complex. She would guess his home security would be good and that he would be prepared if the gang found them at his house. "Does he have any family living with him?"

"Not yet. He's getting married in the spring, but his fiancée lives with her parents right now." Liam got out his cell phone. "Why don't you get what you need and I'll call to ask him?"

Elisabeth unlocked her hard drive and put it in her wall safe. She then packed an overnight bag.

Liam got off the phone. "Nathan said it's fine for us to stay with him. Ready to go?"

She gestured for him to go ahead while she set her alarm. Stepping outside, she found Liam on his back under her car. "Checking for tracking devices," he said.

She had intended to do the same, but was glad to have another set of eyes. "Thanks." She said it awkwardly, not because she wasn't grateful, but because she wasn't used to having someone else help her.

After her car was cleared, she drove around for an hour, with Liam checking behind them to make sure they weren't followed. Remembering what Officer Fong had said about the Bagsics being known for their skilled driving, and the four-car tail that had followed Liam to the women's shelter, it was hard to feel confident that they weren't being tracked. But they couldn't drive around forever—eventually they had to head to their destination.

It was almost dark when they finally turned into a narrow driveway that ended at a horse fence and a low-barred gate. A tall, lean man was already there to swing open the gate and close it behind her car.

Liam rolled down the passenger-side window. "Nathan, nice timing. How'd you know we were coming up the driveway?" The main highway and some lengths of the winding driveway wouldn't be easily visible from the house where it sat between the rolling foothills.

Nathan grinned. "I put in a sensor that warned me when you turned into the driveway from the highway."

"That's handy. Nathan, this is Elisabeth Aday."

Nathan nodded to her, then gestured to the house. "You can park alongside the garage."

The ranch-style home was modest and looked extrasmall sitting in the middle of the generous yard all around it. There was a jungle gym and sandbox beneath a large oak tree in the corner.

"He doesn't have kids, right?" She wouldn't endanger Nathan's family no matter what kind of security he might have.

"Not yet. His fiancée, Arissa, is guardian to her niece. They're still living with Arissa's parents."

When she got out of the car after parking, the winter wind sliced through her sweater. Plucking her laptop case and overnight bag from the backseat where she'd tossed them, she rushed for the front door to the house.

Nathan was already there, holding the door open. "Come on in."

Elisabeth hurried inside the wide foyer and out of the wind, Liam following her. An arched doorway to her right led into a living room.

"Have a seat." Nathan sat in a blue chair in front of a low coffee table holding a carafe and mugs. "Coffee?"

"Please." Elisabeth dropped onto a green sofa opposite

him and set her bags on the floor. Liam dropped into the seat next to her and let out a sigh.

"Want to tell me what's going on?" Nathan poured coffee for them all.

Liam went over what had happened.

"It's safer for you to hide out here." Nathan regarded them with serious green-gray eyes. "You can stay as long as you like."

"We don't want to put you in danger," Elisabeth said.

"If the gang finds you, it's better to have three people against them than just the two of you."

"I needed to talk to you anyway." Liam told him about the SUV of Filipino men who had interrupted the attack by the Bagsics.

Nathan frowned. "There are a couple Filipino gangs in L.A. with tattoos to identify them. You can ask Detective Carter to talk to some of his contacts in San Francisco and Portland, but unless you can draw the tattoo…"

Elisabeth shook her head. "I didn't get a good enough look. I only recognized that the writing was Filipino script. The Bagsics called them Toomies."

"Sounds like a nickname. It could be for a couple different gangs."

"Joe Fong took our statements at Elisabeth's apartment," Liam said. "He told us a bit about the Bagsics. What do you know about them?"

"Not much. They didn't venture into my station's section of Los Angeles very often. I know the other gangs were jealous that their meth trade was doing so well. They dealt out of a few bars and clubs to wealthier customers."

"That reminds me, I had an idea for how to find out more about Joslyn," Elisabeth said.

"I'm guessing you two still have research to do," Nathan said. "You can use the dining room table. You guys hungry?"

Liam grinned. "Always."

Nathan gave them his wireless password and went to fix sandwiches for them as they set up their laptops. As Nathan set the platter of sandwiches in front of them, Liam said, "Thanks. For everything."

Nathan gave a half smile. "Just returning the favor. I'll leave you to it."

Elisabeth stared at Nathan's retreating back, then looked to Liam. "What did he mean by that?"

"Last year, he and his fiancée needed help, and I was able to give it." He suddenly scowled. "Come to think of it, that involved a Filipino gang, too. I must be a magnet or something," he muttered.

Elisabeth didn't pry, although she was dying to. "Back at my apartment, Kayoi's picture gave me an idea. The drawing of the girl with an *S* on her shirt was Joslyn—she probably drew Joslyn since we were all talking about her. I remember that T-shirt. It said *Sayawan,* which means 'dance party' in Tagalog."

Liam's eyebrows rose. "So it was either a fashion statement or…"

"Or maybe a promo item from a club. And Nathan mentioned the Bagsics deal meth out of clubs, right?" Elisabeth opened an internet browser window and began typing. "There's a club in L.A. called Sayawan," she crowed. "Earlier, when I was looking through social media pics, I wasn't paying attention to *where* the photos were taken."

Liam grinned at her. "There's a good chance someone has a picture of Joslyn at the club, especially since she was wearing the T-shirt."

They each took different social media sites and searched for pictures taken at Sayawan. Elisabeth found the picture they wanted almost right away.

It was a shot taken several months ago, with Joslyn smiling into the camera with a handful of friends posing around her. The faces in the photo had been tagged with people's names.

"Joslyn Dimalanta," she said.

"You found her?" Liam left his chair to come look over her shoulder, close enough that she caught a whiff of cedar, and pine, and a lower note of musk. It made her want to close her eyes and breathe it in. She shook off the strange feeling.

"Isn't that that guy in the gray suit from the shelter this morning?" Liam pointed to a man not posing for the picture, but caught in profile in the background.

"It's fuzzy. I can't be sure." She hovered her pointer over the man's face, but he hadn't been tagged.

"Well, at least we've got a place to start." Liam smiled at her, and her vision swirled for a moment before righting itself.

She was relieved when Liam returned to his chair.

"Now that we've got Joslyn's last name, I'll continue to look through social media. You take public records?" she suggested.

"Sure."

Elisabeth looked at who had posted the picture of Joslyn—Esther North. She was very big into photography—usually people, a few nature shots—and according to her photos, she was friends with Joslyn and had seen her several times in the past few months.

Joslyn's own social media had been pretty sparse in the months before she came to Sonoma. She was tagged on some older photos online, but not a lot of recent ones. Which wasn't surprising for a woman in an abusive relationship—many times, the abuser isolated the victim from her old friends. Or she stopped going out because of the bruises.

But Esther had a set of candid photos of Joslyn at a chain electronics store, Perkins Electronics, dressed in an employee's uniform. The photos were artistic shots, as if Esther were practicing taking wedding candid photos. She was taking pictures not only of Joslyn but also of other customers and employees, yet—perhaps because Esther knew Joslyn—the missing woman featured in a larger percentage of the photos.

Esther had caught her at several angles, with several different people who looked like customers. She was smiling in a few of the photos, with a shy tilt to her head and lift of one shoulder.

One photo was a candid of Joslyn speaking to a tall, handsome Filipino man dressed in an expensive gray suit. He was slightly turned away from the camera, but from his partial profile, it seemed he was smiling. Joslyn was clearly smiling up at him.

In the second photo, the two were posing for Esther's camera and the man had his arm around Joslyn a little tighter than a casual acquaintance would hold her.

Elisabeth sucked in a sharp breath. It was the same man in the gray suit from this morning.

Joslyn looked happy. The date was a few months ago, so the photo might have been taken early in their relationship, before Joslyn had discovered what a monster he was.

The two comments below the photo seemed to be from Esther's friends. User BillMP46U seemed to be a photographer because he said, "Cute couple, Esther! Nice way to work around those terrible lights in the store, too!"

The next comment was posted by user Fairydust9437. "Nice photo, Joslyn! Is that Tomas? Wow, he's a cutie."

Elisabeth hovered her pointer over his face to see if he'd been tagged in the photo. He had, but only his first name popped up: Tomas.

"Liam, I think I found him." She swiveled her laptop around so he could see. She couldn't have him standing so close to her again, looking over her shoulder. It did strange things to her breathing.

"Tomas." The name came out from Liam's throat like gravel.

"His clothes are pretty stylish here, too. I think he's higher up in the hierarchy of the gang, a captain or something."

Liam frowned. "Well, I think I found the murder she was talking about." He slid his laptop across the table to her so she could read the website he'd pulled up. "It was buried at the bottom of the fourth or fifth page of search results."

It was a newspaper article from a few weeks ago about a man found brutally beaten and then stabbed to death in his apartment off Silas Avenue. The victim's name was given as Felix Dimalanta, a longtime widower. Police were looking for his missing daughter, Joslyn, who was wanted for questioning.

Her stomach twisted sharply. The murder victim was Joslyn's own father?

The article was brief, barely two paragraphs, and there were no pictures. The report mentioned that the police welcomed any information on the case and that they had talked to Joslyn's coworkers at Perkins Electronics and also to her classmates at Twin Springs College, where she was working to get her computer software engineering degree.

"I didn't know," she whispered. "It never even occurred to me that she might be wanted by the police. All I saw were her bruises."

"When did she arrive at the shelter? How was she, emotionally, when you first saw her?"

"She arrived only a few days after this homicide. There was this…deep grief and horror in her eyes. You could tell she'd recently suffered a terrible blow. I had assumed it was from her last beating, but now I think maybe it was still shock from her father's death." Elisabeth blew out a frustrated breath. "I should have known there was something deeper going on than Joslyn just needing to escape her ex."

"Don't be too hard on yourself. She was injured. Naturally you'd be focused on her safety, not worrying about any type of criminal activity she might have been involved in."

"We really don't yet know how she was involved in her father's murder," Elisabeth said. "He was beaten and then stabbed, so based on her height and frame, it's unlikely Joslyn could have caused that much damage. But did Joslyn witness her father being murdered, as she claimed, or was she involved somehow?"

"To answer that question, we'd have to find out why Tomas killed him. From what I've found about Felix Dimalanta on social media, he didn't have any ties to the Bagsics or any other gang. He didn't have a social media profile, but he had friends who do and they tagged his name on photos."

"Can I see the photos?"

Liam took his laptop back, and after a few clicks of his track pad, gave it to her to look.

Felix Dimalanta had a strong face, a protective set to his shoulders. Elisabeth could see him doing everything as a single parent to care for his daughter and raise her right.

There were photos of him at an inexpensively decorated birthday party, at a couple fast-food restaurants eating with friends, and a cute picture of him riding his bike somewhere and waving to the camera. No photos at upscale restaurants, dressed up for a party or going out to a show.

"He seems to have lived a very modest lifestyle," Elisabeth said.

"The only thing odd about that is his watch."

"His watch?" Elisabeth peered at the photos. He wore the same watch in all the pictures, so it might have been the only watch he owned, the one he used every day.

"I like vintage watches, which is why I noticed it," Liam said. "That's a vintage Rolex—and a pretty valuable one. It might be old enough to have been passed down to Felix by his father. It's the only expensive item he wears, and it's not really the type of watch you'd expect of someone making money from drug deals. So I'm guessing he's not involved in the Bagsics' meth trade."

"Well, Tomas killed him for a reason, and now he's after Joslyn."

"The only way to stop the threat against you and Joslyn is to stop Tomas." Liam had a determined glint in his blue eyes as he held her gaze. "We need to investigate this murder, find evidence and put Tomas in jail."

It was true. Tomas had resources, and he had already shown he absolutely needed Joslyn—and he'd go through Elisabeth to get her. Elisabeth should have been fearful, but instead she was angry and determined. Years ago, she had made a decision that she wouldn't let any man bully her ever again. She would not let Tomas get away with this. "There's only so much we can do with internet research. We have to go to L.A." The heart of Bagsic territory.

Liam's expression was sober. He understood the risks they were taking. "We don't know yet if Tomas told his superiors about you and me in his search for Joslyn. It could be that the gang won't realize Tomas is after us."

At that moment, a distinctive beeping pattern sounded. Within seconds, Nathan appeared, his face tight. "Are you expecting anyone?" he asked abruptly.

"No," Liam answered. "No one even knows we're here."

"Well, I'm not expecting anyone, and that was the sensor for my driveway. Someone's here."

FIVE

Liam shot to his feet. Elisabeth's chest tightened. Had the gang found them somehow?

"We drove around to make sure we weren't followed," Liam said.

"How about a tracker on her car?" Nathan said.

"Liam and I checked my car," Elisabeth said.

"You have about ninety seconds before whoever's headed this way arrives," Nathan said. "What do you want to do?"

Elisabeth grabbed her car keys. "I'll move the car behind the house."

Liam followed her out the door. "I'll hide behind the trees in the yard to wait."

"I'll meet whoever's coming." Nathan stopped to collect a gun from a locked cabinet.

Elisabeth dashed to her car. She cranked the engine and held her breath until it caught. She drove around the house as fast as she could, into a dirt area just beyond the back door.

She pulled her gun from her purse and made her way to the corner of the house, peeking around the edge. She had a clear view of the barred gate, where Nathan stood waiting. His posture was casual, but she could see the tense set of his shoulders even from where she stood. She couldn't see Liam at all, but assumed he was hidden in the shadows of the stand of oak trees.

Soon a car came into view. Elisabeth noted that it was an older-model sedan, nothing like the newer cars that had driven up to the women's shelter. She remained hidden around the corner of the house, but some of the tightness in her stomach relaxed.

Nathan didn't open the gate, but climbed over it to speak to the driver. Elisabeth watched, hating the fact that he was vulnerable to whoever was in the car, despite the fact she knew he was armed. What if the driver pulled a gun, too? She shouldn't have let Nathan greet the visitor by himself.

After a moment, the car did a three-point turn and left. Only then did Elisabeth's jaw unclench. She took a deep breath, then stepped out from behind the corner of the house. Liam appeared next to Nathan at the same time.

"They took a wrong turn," Nathan said. "They were looking for the Howards' farm. It's the next driveway about half a mile down the road."

"It wasn't a trick?" Liam asked.

"Hey." Nathan gave him a mock punch in the arm. "I may not be a detective anymore, but I can still tell when someone's lying."

Liam held his hands up. "Sorry."

They all headed back to the house. "It may have been a false alarm, but it cemented for me that we can't stay here and put you in danger," Elisabeth said.

Nathan opened the front door for them. "I can take care of myself, and I can help you. Besides, there's strength in numbers."

"Not if we have to stay out of sight because we're not supposed to be here," Elisabeth said. "Just now, we left you exposed. And what if someone comes to visit you and gets caught up in our mess, too?"

"She's right." Liam's eyes were determined as they

rested on his friend. "When you and Arissa and Charity stayed at my place last year, I didn't have any visitors because no one in Sonoma knew yet that I'd come back to town. But you have a job here, friends, family. You're not as isolated as I was. Having us hide out here is more dangerous to you."

Nathan closed the front door, his jaw set stubbornly.

"Besides, we have to go to Los Angeles," Elisabeth said.

"Because it's so much safer to go somewhere crawling with Bagsics," Nathan said.

"We need to find a way to stop the threat against Elisabeth and Joslyn," Liam said.

"We think Joslyn's ex-boyfriend, who looks like he might be a Bagsic captain, murdered her father," Elisabeth said. "If we can find proof, we can put him in jail and the threat against us will end."

"We were hoping you could check with your LAPD contacts for information about the murder," Liam added. "In the meantime…we're investigators. We'll investigate down in L.A."

Nathan hesitated, then reluctantly nodded. "I'll give my contacts a call and see if I can dig up anything that'll point you in the right direction. But you'll need to be careful with your investigating. You won't have a chance to find much if you're recognized by the gang."

"I have an idea," Elisabeth said. "But I'll need some help."

Jericho Street was crawling with Bagsic gang members.

Liam's palms were damp against the steering wheel, but he tried to keep his posture casual as he drove Elisabeth's car down the residential Los Angeles street. Every block or so, Liam spotted a Bagsic member in purple and gray.

"That's her address." Elisabeth pointed to an apartment building with dingy walls painted Pepto-Bismol pink.

Joslyn's official place of residence was her father's apartment. On the six-hour drive down from Northern California this morning, Elisabeth had called the three places in Los Angeles that she knew referred women to Sonoma's Wings shelter. One had been an Asian-American church, which was nearby Joslyn's father's apartment. In speaking to the women's ministry staff worker, Elisabeth had discovered that one of the church members, Mrs. Andrada, lived in the same apartment building as Joslyn's father. So that was their first stop.

The building only had street parking, which was full. They would have to park down the street and walk, passing Bagsic members on the sidewalk.

Liam glanced at Elisabeth. "You ready?"

She ran her hands down her newly curled hair, lightened to dark blond from its normal deep brown. "I think so. I guess this will be a test to see if the Los Angeles Bagsics were given our pictures or not."

"Even if they were given our pictures, they wouldn't recognize you now." Nathan had asked his fiancée, Arissa, to pick up items to help Elisabeth disguise herself, changing not just her hair but her eyes with light-colored contact lenses from a costume store, which transformed Elisabeth's golden-hazel eyes to green. Elisabeth had spent part of the night lightening and perming her hair, and she now looked more Caucasian than Filipino.

"I know you said you met Patricia at an outdoor café, while wearing sunglasses, but do you really think that baseball cap is going to disguise you enough?" Elisabeth asked him.

He tugged the bill farther down his forehead. "It hides my buzz cut and my eyes. Do I need more makeup?" Arissa had also gotten a dark shade of makeup, which Elisabeth applied to Liam's face, neck, and exposed hands to darken his already tanned skin tone.

"No, any more and you'll look odd with your facial hair." At her suggestion, he hadn't shaved, and his golden-brown whiskers, which always grew quickly, now softened his jawline. It would take a day or two to be a more effective disguise. He was reminded why he preferred to be clean-shaven when he had to constantly stop himself from scratching at it.

He parallel-parked two blocks from the building. There was a spot closer to the apartment, but it had been next to an expensive BMW coupe with a couple Bagsic members leaning against the car.

As they got out of the car, Liam casually scanned the street. The weather was a bit warmer down here in Southern California, but the winter chill still cut through his leather jacket. Christmas lights were strung in apartment windows, and a few doors sported small wreaths. He compared the tired-looking decorations to his father's home, lavishly decorated with lawn ornaments, beribboned wreaths, and dripping with Christmas lights.

Elisabeth headed down the sidewalk, her stride confident. Liam hurried to catch up to her. He admired how she tended to attack obstacles as if conquering a hill, but it also made him want to protect her and shield her, which he knew she wouldn't appreciate.

Her pace faltered as they were forced to pass the two Bagsic members leaning against the BMW. One had a more aggressive posture and wasn't as finely dressed as the other, who looked more like a Bagsic captain.

The captain's mouth pulled into a slow, predatory smile as Elisabeth approached, and Liam's hands in his jacket pockets clenched into fists. The man's dark eyes roved over Elisabeth's body, conservatively dressed in jeans, boots and a black wool peacoat. Elisabeth stiffened for a second, but then she gave him a saucy smile, lifted a shoulder as she passed him and tossed her hair before continuing on her way.

Liam had to concentrate to relax his stiff jaw. "What was that about?" he growled to her.

She muttered back to him, "Those guys are used to women fawning over them. Ignoring him would have gotten his attention. Now I'm just one of dozens of girls he'll see today."

Liam hadn't thought of that. He'd only felt the need to protect her. He risked a look behind him and saw the two men climb into their car, which soon headed down the street.

They climbed the cracked cement steps to the apartment building and found the back stairs to the second floor. The landing was surprisingly clean. Joslyn's father's apartment was cordoned off with yellow police tape. The door looked as though it had been kicked in, and a padlock had been put in place. There was a small window beside the door, but the curtain prevented them from seeing much.

"I wish we could go in," she said.

"Unless you'd like to add breaking and entering to your police rap sheet…"

She sighed. "Absolutely not." She knocked on the door directly across.

Mrs. Andrada, who answered the door, was a small woman, frail looking with sad eyes and a droopy mouth. Her short hair was beautifully curly and snow-white, and she gazed up at them with slightly clouded brown eyes. "Yes?"

"Mrs. Andrada, I'm Elisabeth Aday and this is Liam O'Neill. We spoke on the phone?"

"Oh, yes, come in." Her Filipino accent was very slight. She stepped aside.

The living room they entered was shabby but scrupulously clean. Mrs. Andrada was apparently partial to lime-green and sunflower-yellow, because the colors popped up in the print of the sofa, the pictures on the wall and the throw rugs that brightened the thin beige carpet. The windows were thrown wide-open, making the apartment cold, but it seemed to be airing out the faint scent of bananas and frying oil that he could smell.

"Sit." Mrs. Andrada gestured to the sofa. "Do you like *lumpiyang saging?*"

Liam blinked, not sure what he had heard.

"Love it," Elisabeth said enthusiastically. As Mrs. Andrada disappeared through a narrow doorway into the tiny kitchen, Elisabeth leaned close to Liam and whispered, "Bananas in a deep-fried spring roll."

"Oh." That explained the smell.

Mrs. Andrada served them the small fried spring rolls alongside a sweet, hot, strong ginger tea that woke him up as effectively as coffee. The spring rolls were still warm, crispy on the outside and filled with sweet bananas.

Elisabeth leaned forward, her hands around the cracked mug holding her ginger tea. "Mrs. Andrada, as I mentioned on the phone, we're trying to help Joslyn."

"Isn't Joslyn at Wings shelter? I told her about it."

"I'm afraid she left Wings a few weeks ago."

Mrs. Andrada sighed and leaned back in her comfortable recliner, decorated with a green-and-yellow crocheted blanket thrown over the back. "I'm so worried about that girl. I used to babysit her when she was little, you know? I knew her boyfriend was bad news."

"Did you know Joslyn's boyfriend, too?"

The woman shook her head. "I never met him. That's how I knew he was wrong for her. She and her father had such a close relationship, and her boyfriend never came by to meet him."

Through the open window came the sound of raised

men's voices speaking in Filipino. Both Elisabeth and Mrs. Andrada's brows wrinkled at whatever they were saying.

"Is something wrong?" Liam asked.

"Not really," Elisabeth said. "I guess I'm just jumpy with so many Bagsics nearby."

"One of them sounds like Mrs. Navarro's boy." Mrs. Andrada sighed. "She didn't want him involved with any of the gangs, but living in this neighborhood, it's hard for the kids not be influenced."

Liam rose and went to look out the window. There were some young gang members, and they were congregating around a souped-up Accord parked along the street. They weren't quite arguing, but it wasn't a gentle discussion, either. He remained by the window, watching them, as Elisabeth continued talking to Mrs. Andrada.

"Did Joslyn ever talk to you about Tomas?" Elisabeth asked.

"She was always so shy, she didn't date many men. Stupid." Mrs. Andrada said something in Filipino. "Joslyn is so beautiful. So when she first started dating Tomas, I was pleased for her because she seemed so happy. She moved in with him and stopped visiting her father as often. But then later in the relationship, she started visiting her papa more, and she seemed very subdued whenever I saw her. I kept praying for her, and then one day she confessed that Tomas beat her. He kept her from her friends at work and school. He'd only let her come visit her papa."

Liam couldn't stop the fire that flared in his gut as he heard about what Tomas had done to Joslyn. Even his isolating her from her friends was a form of abuse. He couldn't stand men like that, who wanted to feel superior by taking advantage of someone weaker. Even the young gang members outside seemed to be picking on the smallest and youngest, a slender boy who couldn't be more than fifteen years old.

"A few days after that, Joslyn pounded on my door. She was covered in blood and distraught. Her papa was dead and she was so afraid." Mrs. Andrada shuddered. "She said that Tomas and his friends had killed her papa because he wouldn't tell them where she was." Mrs. Andrada sniffed, reaching for tissues in a box next to her. She dabbed her eyes. "He was such a good man."

Liam looked away from the window for a moment. "He wasn't involved with the Bagsics, was he?"

"No," Mrs. Andrada said emphatically. "He didn't even know Joslyn's boyfriend was a Bagsic captain, although she told me."

"Do you remember the time Joslyn came to your apartment after her father was killed?" Liam asked.

Mrs. Andrada pursed her lips as she thought back. "I had just started watching *Survivor* when she came in."

Liam nodded. It would be easy to look at a TV schedule and figure out about what time Joslyn had come to Mrs. Andrada.

"How awful for Joslyn." Elisabeth's voice was soft. "To be betrayed by her boyfriend and then to lose her father, all at once."

"She felt more frightened than betrayed by Tomas," Mrs. Andrada said. "They stole her father's money and all his valuables, making it look like a robbery gone wrong. Joslyn was scared because Tomas was after her. So I told her about Wings shelter in Sonoma, because I knew they'd keep her safe." The woman's lower lip trembled. "I wish I could have done more for her. Why did she leave that shelter?"

Elisabeth shook her head. "I don't know. She was very frightened of Tomas. I think she was afraid he'd find her, and then it would endanger everyone else at the shelter."

Mrs. Andrada nodded slowly. "She was like that, thinking about others. She said she stopped seeing her friends because she didn't want Tomas to know about them."

"Did she think they'd get involved in the gang, too?"

"No. I think she was afraid Tomas might use them against her somehow, if he knew how much they meant to her."

Like her father.

"Did you know any of her friends?" Elisabeth asked.

"I only know one girl, Mariella Gable. A very nice Chinese girl. She brought me moon cakes for Chinese New Year." Mrs. Andrada's face creased as she smiled. "She and Joslyn were both studying for their master's degrees at the college."

Liam straightened as he continued watching the men on the street. The argument seemed to be getting heated.

"You won't mention anything that I've told you to the Bagsics, will you?" Mrs. Andrada wrung her hands together, the tendons standing out under her frail skin. "This neighborhood is part of their territory."

"We won't say anything about you." Elisabeth reached forward and laid her hand over the woman's fingers.

"My son would tell me not to get involved with Felix's murder, but he was my friend for so many years. And anyway, I can't do nothing while Joslyn is in danger."

"We're doing everything we can to put Tomas in jail," Elisabeth said fiercely. "Can you tell us anything more about him?"

The woman shook her head. "He never came here except the day he killed Felix."

"Do you know where he lives?" Liam asked. They knew so little about Tomas and the night of the murder, and while his neighbors might be afraid, they might speak to Elisabeth and Liam because they weren't cops. Yet that was only a possibility if they could find the building.

"No, though it wasn't far. Joslyn would mention it only

took a few minutes to drive here from his apartment building."

But in this section of L.A., there were dozens of apartment buildings all within twenty minutes from this street. How could they know which direction? Would they have to visit all of them?

"Did Joslyn ever give you any gifts?" Elisabeth asked.

Liam looked at her. What an odd question.

"Gifts? Like Christmas?" Mrs. Andrada asked.

"Little things, like candy, or a trinket."

"Oh, yes." Mrs. Andrada got up and went to a small card table in the corner of the living room, returning with a flat pastry box. "I like the mochi from Oishii Bakery, so she would bring me some whenever she called. My son brought me some yesterday. Did you want one?"

Liam tentatively tried one of the small rice cake balls. The glutinous rice on the outside was soft and sticky, while the inside was filled with sweet red bean paste.

"Mmm." Elisabeth licked the sticky remnants from her fingers. "Did Joslyn give you anything else?"

Mrs. Andrada thought a moment. "She did once give me roast pork from Elena's Filipino Restaurant. And for Christmas she brought me this." Mrs. Andrada rose and returned with a green pashmina shawl, which still had the tag on it. "It's so fine, I don't have anywhere to wear it."

Elisabeth glanced at the tag. "Theo's Boutique."

The men's voices from outside carried clearly into the living room. Liam didn't have to understand Filipino to know they were now in a heated argument—and they were only a few feet away from Elisabeth's car.

"I don't like the sound of that," Mrs. Andrada said. "You should go before it gets worse. They're such hotheads...."

Elisabeth rose to her feet. "Thank you for speaking to us."

"Just do what you can to keep Joslyn safe." Mrs. Andrada squeezed Elisabeth's hands briefly.

As Liam and Elisabeth stepped out onto the sidewalk, he pulled her in the opposite direction from their car and the arguing gang members. "Let's circle around and come up to the car from the other direction."

"You don't need to convince me." She hurried alongside him, away from the rapid-fire Filipino that was steadily rising in volume.

By the time they turned the corner, they saw that the argument had petered out, but the men had migrated closer to where they were parked.

An old pickup truck headed down the street, its engine chugging and sputtering. And suddenly there was a loud, sharp *bang!*

In an instant, the street dissolved into arid desert, grit in Liam's mouth, sun and sweat in his eyes. Voices shouting, gunfire in loud bursts all around him. His heartbeat rapid and hard against his chest, squeezing his lungs so he couldn't breathe. There were men all around him, jerking and falling, bleeding into the dirt and sand. He was going to die if he didn't fire his weapon, but he couldn't lift his arm. There was too much pain sizzling up his shoulder like acid. He realized he was on the ground, and the blood in the sand was his own. Men around him were shouting, saying—

"Liam!"

The low, feminine voice throbbed in his ear. His eyes came into focus abruptly, uncomfortably. Green eyes were in front of him, close to his face.

"Liam, you're all right." Elisabeth's voice soothed him, calmed his galloping heartbeat. He wasn't in Afghanistan anymore. He was in Los Angeles.

His legs trembled, and he noticed he was leaning back heavily against a car. Elisabeth's hands were gentle on his shoulder, the side of his face. He gulped in air, cold with the California winter and not hot and dry from the desert.

"Hey, what's wrong with him?"

The man's voice cut through the dissolving remnants of his waking nightmare. The Bagsics. They had been directly in front of him when he'd…

Elisabeth turned to look at him, and while her face was passive, Liam could feel her hands were tense. "He's fine," she said to them.

"He don't look fine." And then the Bagsics started walking toward them.

There were four of them. None looked over twenty-one years old, and their purple and gray clothes looked inexpensive.

One of the others said something to her in Filipino. She pretended she didn't understand, but her eyes, so close to Liam, froze.

Liam's muscles bunched up. What had the boy said? They were coming closer.

"Troy Navarro!" a woman's voice called sharply from the direction of the apartment building. "Does your mother know where you are?"

Liam was surprised to see Mrs. Andrada at the front of the apartment building, hands on her hips, glaring at the young men. The youngest, the fifteen-year-old, immediately hunched his shoulders, while his friends gave him sly nudges and said what sounded like derisive remarks in Filipino. It also distracted them from Elisabeth and Liam.

"Come on," she hissed. She shoved him into the passenger seat of her car.

Liam looked back as Elisabeth drove away. Mrs. Andrada headed back into the apartment building while the gang members drifted away, several of them still teasing the fifteen-year-old.

Elisabeth's sigh of relief was shaky. "They were just punks looking for trouble."

"Did they recognize you?"

"No. I didn't think they would. They're not high up in the gang hierarchy, and a gang captain like Tomas wouldn't publicize his private business."

"What did he say to you?" Liam clenched and unclenched his hands in his lap. He'd been so useless, so helpless.

She shook her head. "Nothing nice."

She didn't make a fuss over the way he'd fallen apart. She was so understanding and caring. He didn't want her to be. He didn't want to suck anyone else into the dark madness of his mind. And he couldn't afford to be like this when Elisabeth was depending on him. "This is too dangerous," he muttered.

"We knew it was going to be dangerous," she said. "But there's no safe way to investigate the murder. And really, we're just being antsy. The gang members didn't treat us any differently from anyone else they see on the street."

He knew she was right, but he didn't like it. And the worst part was, he could only expect things to get worse.

SIX

Elisabeth didn't want to take any chances. She drove out of Bagsic territory until she found a coffee shop with free wireless internet and no sign of men in purple and gray. As she sipped her coffee, she carefully watched their surroundings while Liam looked up Mariella Gable and the three shops Mrs. Andrada had mentioned. She had to admit that Liam was a great deal faster at finding Mariella's information on the internet than she would have been. They would make a good—

No, she wasn't going down that road again.

The coffee shop was busy with students from nearby Twin Springs College. No gang members appeared. It could have been a normal day, without the threat to her life.

Normal for her usually meant helping the women at the shelter, doing her job. Her job took up all her time— or rather, she spent all her time at her job, working on her own. She was…comfortable with her life. She was alone and comfortable. She didn't need anyone else. She didn't need anything else but herself.

She looked at Liam, his head bent over his computer. He glanced up at her and flashed her a brief smile.

That smile transformed him. His dark blue eyes crinkled, his mouth was relaxed and gentle rather than hard and serious. He looked…trustworthy.

Elisabeth looked away.

His cell phone rang, and he glanced at the caller ID. "Nathan."

Hopefully he had some information for them about Tomas and Joslyn's father's murder.

Nathan talked to his friend, giving mmm-hmm's and asking the occasional question. Finally he said, "Thanks, Nathan," and disconnected the call. "Sorry I didn't put it on speakerphone, but..."

He wouldn't want their conversation to be overheard. "I understand. What did he say?"

"Tomas Bantoc is known to be a high-ranking captain in the Bagsic gang. He has some anger issues, but can usually control them, which makes him ruthless and effective."

"That means either something made him lose it when he killed Joslyn's father, or he had a compelling reason."

"Like Mrs. Andrada said, she called the police after Joslyn left. Joslyn's father had been tied to a chair, beaten and then stabbed to death."

Elisabeth closed her eyes briefly at the brutal image. What would the sight of her bloody, lifeless father have made Joslyn feel? Elisabeth's heart ached for her.

"The police found out about Joslyn's relationship with Tomas and went to question him, but Tomas claimed he'd been at Sayawan at the time of the murder."

Elisabeth shared a quick look with Liam. "The same club where we found the pictures of Joslyn."

"The police didn't find any evidence that Joslyn was involved in the actual crime, but they still want to speak to her," Liam said. "They alerted other agencies about her, and a policeman in central California filed a report the day after Joslyn's father's murder. He saw Joslyn exiting a bus at a small stop just outside of Paso Robles, but she must have realized she'd been recognized and disappeared.

Her ticket had been for San Francisco, but she never got back on the bus."

"And no other sightings of her?"

"Nope."

Elisabeth chewed her lip. "Would a gang captain really bother to find one woman who knows about a murder but doesn't have proof?"

"There's some reason he's after her—maybe the reason why he attacked her father in the first place. Gang captains are powerful. They wouldn't exert themselves unless there's a pressing reason."

"So we keep digging into Tomas."

"Murder is a capital offense in California. If we can uncover proof against him, Tomas might turn on the Bagsics in order to escape the death penalty. Nathan said he saw it happen several times with other gang members when he was down south." Liam closed his laptop. "Let's get out of here. I feel exposed."

Elisabeth got in the car, which was parked along the street in front of the coffee shop, and cranked the engine. "Was I right about the three shops?"

"Yup, they're all close to each other. I found three apartment buildings in that area, but the one to check first is Hamilton Towers. It's the most expensive, and the only one with a gated underground garage, which a Bagsic captain would appreciate."

"Good thinking." Elisabeth followed Liam's directions and parked near Hamilton Towers, an imposing building with four floors, all chrome, glass and gray concrete.

As they got out, Elisabeth caught sight of the security cameras outside the front door. "There are probably security guards inside. How are we going to get past them to question Tomas's neighbors?" Elisabeth said.

At that moment, the doors were opened by a doorman in a uniform. He must have been standing just inside the door. He nodded rather solemnly to two men who were walking out of the building.

They were dressed in purple and gray.

Elisabeth's first reaction was to freeze, but she forced herself to relax, knowing the gang members would catch any sign of fear. She had known a predator before, and she knew if she didn't put up a perfectly unconcerned facade, the gang members would start to circle around her.

She glanced at them idly, and realized they were the same gang members that they'd seen on Jericho Street, leaning against the BMW coupe. Her breath hitched and she tried to even it out. This was not good.

The man in the purple silk shirt was saying to the other in Tagalog, "No, I don't want to take my car. I just got it washed and it might rain later today."

"They're the same—" Liam murmured.

"I know." Her back was to the two men, but she could hear their footfalls on the sidewalk.

"You look familiar."

Her jaw tightened at the sound of the man's voice. She relaxed her face into an innocent mask and half turned, regarding him from over her shoulder.

The gang member in the silk shirt had stopped and was appraising her exactly the same way he'd done before.

Elisabeth answered lightly, "I saw you on Jericho Street. I was visiting a friend."

She was about to turn her head back around when he asked, "So what are you doing here?"

She hesitated only a split second. "We're looking at different apartment buildings." As she turned to face him, she thrust her hips out and put her hand directly over her stomach. With her thick wool peacoat, she knew she looked like she could be a few months pregnant.

His face cooled into an almost disdainful expression,

and she knew she'd read him correctly. He relished his single lifestyle, and children were a complete turnoff.

At that moment, a man and woman exited the apartment building. In contrast to how he had treated the two Bagsics, the doorman said jovially, "Have a good day, Mr. and Mrs. Alfred."

"Thanks, Samuel," the woman said.

The couple headed toward them, but as soon as they saw the two Bagsics, their steps quickened and they hurried by, heads down and shoulders hunched. They apparently knew their gang-affiliated neighbors and wanted nothing to do with them.

"Do you and your friend live here?" Elisabeth asked, playing her part.

"I do, he doesn't." The man in the silk shirt seemed almost reluctant to answer, now that he had no interest in her. "They only give you one parking space in the garage. One of you will have to park on the street."

"Oh." She gave a moue of distaste. "Thanks."

The two men walked away and soon drove off.

Liam blew out his breath. "I can't believe you talked to them."

"It would have looked odd if I hadn't."

"Did you see those people who walked past? The gang has them running scared."

Elisabeth sighed. If that couple was any indication, the other residents were clearly afraid of their gang neighbors and would probably be reluctant to talk to Elisabeth and Liam.

"I have an idea." She marched up to the front door. The doorman had disappeared and the front door was locked, so she pushed a doorbell button. A small door to the side of the elevators marked Security opened and the doorman, Samuel, hurried toward them. "Yes?" he asked through the closed glass door.

Elisabeth studied his face. She had noticed his different reactions to the Bagsics and to the couple, and she trusted her instincts about people. "My name is Elisabeth Aday, and this is Liam O'Neill. We're not police, we're investigators. We're trying to protect Joslyn Dimalanta from her ex-boyfriend, Tomas Bantoc."

Samuel's face tightened, and his eyes shifted to the street behind them, looking left and right.

"Please, will you let us in? We only want to talk to you. We're not here to get anyone in trouble with the gang."

The doorman hesitated, then pushed open the door to let them into the foyer.

"Thanks." Elisabeth and Liam slipped inside.

"This way." Samuel glanced out to the street once again, then headed to the security room.

There was only one chair, but Samuel pulled out a folding chair for Elisabeth, and Liam stood and leaned against the closed door.

Samuel sat, resting his hands on his thighs. "Tell me what you want with Joslyn."

"A few weeks ago, I helped her to disappear," Elisabeth said. "All I knew at the time was that she was scared and running from her ex-boyfriend, who beat her. But then Tomas came looking for her, and now he's after me to get me to tell him where she is."

Samuel leaned forward. "Is she all right?"

"As far as I know."

"We think she ran because she saw Tomas murder her father," Liam said. "If we can find proof Tomas killed him, we can send him to jail and he won't be a threat to her anymore."

Samuel nodded slowly, his eyes downcast. "I read about the murder in the paper, and I've been worried about that girl ever since."

"Is there anything you can tell us about what happened?" Liam asked.

"Or anything about Joslyn and Tomas?" Elisabeth added. There may be things he didn't think were significant that might help them find the proof they needed.

"Well, the day of the murder, one of Tomas's neighbors called to complain that Tomas and Joslyn were having a huge fight and something hit the wall, causing a crack on their side of the wall."

"Did they fight a lot?" Liam asked.

"All the time, but this was the first time they'd caused damage. I went up to Tomas's apartment, but I must have missed Joslyn because she wasn't there anymore. Tomas still looked angry."

"When was this?" Liam asked.

"Let's see…I have to record any disturbances in the log." Samuel pulled out a three-ring binder. He flipped through the pages and found the entry, which listed the time as three hours before the murder.

"The next day, the papers mentioned Joslyn's father had been killed. As soon as I saw that, I went back to look at the security video feed. Joslyn came back to Tomas's apartment five hours after she left, and when she left the apartment, it looked like she was stuffing cash into her purse."

"Cash?" But Joslyn had arrived in Sonoma only two days later with no money and no purse.

Samuel sighed. "I know it makes her look bad, stealing money from her boyfriend, but I saw her bruises, day in and day out. I'm just glad she finally got away from him."

"Can we see the video?" Liam asked.

Samuel shook his head. "The police took it when they came around to talk to Tomas. They didn't arrest him."

Elisabeth asked, "Do you think we could talk to Tomas's neighbors?"

"No," Samuel said quickly. "It'll cost me my job if I let

you upstairs to knock on people's doors. Plus, no one will talk to you about Tomas. They're all too afraid of the gang. There's at least two other Bagsics living here."

Elisabeth chewed on her lip. "You can't think of anyone who might speak to us?"

"I guarantee that none of his neighbors or friends will say anything."

Samuel was so emphatic, Elisabeth didn't doubt him. As they thanked him and got up to leave, she reflected that while *Tomas's* friends certainly wouldn't say anything, *Joslyn's* friends might.

Mrs. Andrada had told them about Joslyn's friend, Mariella Gable. Would she know something about Joslyn or Tomas that would unlock some form of proof about the murder?

Liam initially thought Mariella Gable's apartment building was outside of Bagsic territory—until he spotted two young men in purple and gray loitering outside the nearby urgent care clinic. Liam turned his head away as they drove past the men.

"I'll try to find parking farther from them." Liam turned the car down a side street.

Easier said than done. However, he finally managed to find a spot in a tiny city-owned public parking lot several blocks from the clinic and Mariella's home.

"If we weren't trying to avoid them, I probably wouldn't notice the number of Bagsics on the street." Liam took a quick look around the full parking lot as he got out of the car.

"I'm still not convinced you're fully disguised." Elisabeth studied Liam, her eyes roving over his face and neck. "I might need to reapply your makeup later."

Liam shrugged. "My guess is that only captains or higher know about me and my connection to you and

Joslyn. And the captain we've seen so far today didn't look twice at me."

That could have been because the man had been too busy flirting with Elisabeth. A muscle in Liam's jaw spasmed briefly.

As they headed down the sidewalk, Liam noticed how the wind had picked up and the sky had clouded over. There was the smell of cold ozone, although it hadn't yet started to rain.

They turned the corner and headed toward Mariella's building. Liam glanced briefly to where they'd last seen the two Bagsics, but they had disappeared.

The building was older but well cared for. They pressed the buzzer for Mariella's apartment and waited, then pressed it again. After the third time, he said, "Sounds like she's not home."

"She might still be on campus."

As they walked back down the sidewalk toward the car, a gust of wind tugged at the brim of his baseball cap. His hand was tangled in his jacket pocket, and before he could reach up to grab it, his cap flew off his head.

He whipped around and snatched it up off the sidewalk. As he straightened and turned around, however, he looked up.

Several yards ahead of them, on the sidewalk, were three Bagsics who had just come out of the urgent care clinic. One of them had his arm in a sling. His face also showed signs of bruising. At that moment, he looked directly into Liam's face.

It was the hotheaded gang member. The one Liam had struggled with at Wings shelter in Sonoma.

And he recognized Liam at the same time. "Hey!"

The men were in between Liam and Elisabeth and the car. "Come on!" He pulled her back and they ran down the sidewalk.

He must have driven back to L.A. from Sonoma after the fight at the shelter. It made sense that he'd go to this urgent care clinic, since it was relatively near Bagsic territory.

"Let's cut through here." Liam took a sharp right down an alley that looked as if it would lead them back to the car. He looked over his shoulder and slowed when he saw Elisabeth had fallen behind, but she waved him on.

"Go! Start the car!" she shouted.

He sprinted ahead along the twisting alley. He turned another corner and could see the street up ahead.

A body barreled into him, slamming him onto the ground. His cheek scraped against gravel, and he could taste dirt and motor oil. He kicked out at the weight against his lower limbs, and his foot connected with something soft. He heard a low "Oof!"

Liam had been going to the gym since returning stateside, at first for his physical therapy, but then to train in mixed martial arts. He recalled the drills he'd learned from his coach and whipped out again with his foot, catching his attacker sharply on the side of one knee. The man cried out in pain and fell hard, clutching his knee, while Liam sprang to his feet.

He brought his hands up in time to block a punch from a second gang member. The man's technique was precise— he'd been trained in fighting.

Liam delivered a few jabs that didn't connect, then faked a left fist and shot out with a right punch. It connected with the man's jaw, and he staggered backward but didn't fall. Liam pursued him, but the man brought his arms up to block him.

Several solid blows to the man's torso made the gang member curl inward, and Liam took the opening to grasp the back of the man's neck and slam it down into his knee. The attacker crumpled to the ground.

Liam whirled, looking for the third man, who had been injured. He saw Elisabeth standing over the man's inert form, clasping a short length of wood she must have picked up from the alleyway. She was breathing heavily.

"Are you all right?" Liam asked. His heart still slammed fast and hard against his chest from the fight.

She nodded. Her face was pale, but she looked strong and determined rather than frightened.

"Let's get out of here." Liam put his hand out and she took it. Her fingers trembled slightly, but she squeezed his hand.

They ran down the alley toward the street. They slowed when they reached the sidewalk, but walked quickly to the car. Liam kept a firm grip on Elisabeth's hand, his eyes scanning the street for any more Bagsic members. Fortunately, they saw no more purple and gray as they climbed into the car and sped away.

"Oh, Liam." Elisabeth's eyes were pained. "We should have tried to disguise you better."

"How? A decent wig would have been too hard to get at such short notice, and that man might have recognized me anyway. He got a good look at me when we were struggling at Wings shelter."

"This only makes things harder for us."

Liam knew she was right. Because now the Bagsic gang would know that Liam was in Los Angeles.

SEVEN

"You should have stayed in the car," Elisabeth hissed to Liam as they walked toward Twin Springs College's computer sciences building.

"I heard you the first three times." Liam's head swiveled left and right as he tracked the students who crisscrossed the large quad in the center of campus. "I'm not leaving you alone."

"It's more dangerous for you now that the Bagsics know you're in L.A."

"It's just as dangerous for you to be alone. There's a good chance they've figured out who you are, too."

Elisabeth wasn't entirely sure why she was more worried about Liam than herself. Perhaps because she was becoming accustomed to working with him. He listened to her, he respected her. He also argued with her, like he was doing now, motivated by his desire to do the right thing.

Liam opened one of the two wooden double doors to the computer sciences building and they walked into the front foyer. A young woman at the front desk looked up at them. "Can I help you?"

Elisabeth hesitated. The college wouldn't simply give information on one of their students to complete strangers, but since Mariella wasn't at home, there was a good chance she was still at school, maybe in class or in a lab.

She smiled at the receptionist. "I'm looking for a TA, Mariella Gable?"

"I don't have TA office hours here at the front desk, but they should be posted on the bulletin board just down the hall there, along with her office number and telephone number." The receptionist pointed down a main hallway that ran behind the desk toward the back of the building.

"Thanks." Elisabeth let out a long breath as she and Liam walked down the hallway.

"How did you know Mariella was a TA?" Liam asked in a low voice.

"I didn't. It was a desperation play. I figured that there was a good chance that a student in the master's program would also be a teaching assistant."

"Nice." He smiled at her, and as it had before, that smile made her stomach flutter.

Elisabeth forced her attention to the bulletin board, searching for Mariella's name, and she gasped. "She really *is* a TA. Her office hours ended twenty minutes ago."

"She might still be here." Liam took off down the hallway at a run, but he slowed to look back at her. "Come on."

They sprinted up several sets of carpeted stairs to the fifth floor. Liam got to the office door first and rapped sharply on the wood. Elisabeth, who had never been a strong runner, tried to get her breathing under control, a bit annoyed that Liam barely looked as though his heart rate had risen.

The door didn't have a window in it, so there was no way to tell if Mariella had left already. They waited, and Liam knocked again.

This time, the door swung open to reveal an Asian woman talking on her cell phone. She held up a finger to them to indicate she'd be with them in a moment. "Yes, please change the appointment to next Thursday.…Three-thirty is fine.…Great, thanks." She disconnected the call and said to Liam and Elisabeth, "Sorry, office hours are over for today."

"We're not students," Liam said. "We were hoping to speak to you about your friend, Joslyn Dimalanta."

Mariella's expression didn't obviously change, but she grew very, very still. "And who are you?"

"I'm Liam O'Neill. I'm a skip tracer. This is Elisabeth Aday, a private investigator. We're trying to protect Joslyn by investigating her ex-boyfriend."

Mariella's dark eyes grew fierce. "Come in." She closed the door behind them.

Elisabeth and Liam sat in the two chairs opposite Mariella's desk, which looked as if a computer had exploded on top of it. "Tomas is an animal," Mariella said. "The things he did to Joslyn…"

"We have reason to believe he killed Joslyn's father." Liam explained about Joslyn arriving in Sonoma and disappearing soon after Elisabeth had helped her, and everything they'd learned about the homicide.

"You have to make the police put Tomas away for good." Mariella's brows drew low over her eyes, which Elisabeth could see, in the light from the window, were brown streaked with green. She must have some Caucasian blood in addition to her Asian ancestry.

"We're still looking for more information about what happened the night of the murder," Liam said. "He told the police he was at a club at the time."

"Which club? Sayawan?"

"Yes, do you know it?" Elisabeth asked.

"Joslyn and I went there sometimes after computer lab on Friday nights. Tomas has probably got five or six gang members willing to lie and give him an alibi."

"We haven't been able to find any proof otherwise," Liam said.

Mariella's mouth grew firm. "I know how you can find

proof. My cousin Dawn works at Sayawan as a waitress. She would be able to tell you who was there that night."

Excitement started to rise in Elisabeth's chest. "Do you have her phone number? We can call to ask if we can stop by her home."

Mariella shook her head. "You won't want to talk to Dawn at her apartment. Dawn's roommate has Bagsic ties—it's how Dawn got her job at Sayawan."

Elisabeth began chewing on her lip. Even if they talked to Dawn over the phone, there was a chance her roommate might overhear the conversation. "Maybe we could speak to her at work?"

"It would be easiest to talk to her at the club." There was a strange light in Mariella's eyes. "No one notices if a waitress is talking to a couple customers."

"But there will be Bagsic members in the club."

"They won't be paying attention if you seem like normal customers. If you talk to her at her apartment, even on the street, someone will see you speaking to her and she might get in trouble with the gang."

"We should go tonight, before those Bagsics have more time to tell people they saw me," Liam said. "We'll get disguises."

"You probably won't get in," Mariella said. "Men have to wait in line, whereas all the young women get in right away."

"I'm not letting you go in alone," Liam said in a forceful voice. His blue eyes bored into Elisabeth, and she was hit with the full force of his determination.

"It's a lot easier for me to change my appearance drastically with makeup and a haircut," Elisabeth said.

"You won't be alone, because I'll go in with you," Mariella said.

Liam and Elisabeth both paused their arguing to stare at Mariella.

"It's too dangerous—" Elisabeth said at the same time that Liam said, "No way."

Mariella's eyes flattened. "I'll have you know that I've been studying wushu martial arts since I was a child, and I can take care of myself. Just last week, I sparred against four attackers at once."

Elisabeth had known another woman trained in wushu. She had been both graceful and formidable as an opponent.

"Dawn will also probably be more willing to talk to you if I'm there," Mariella said. "And now that I know about Tomas's alibi, I'm going in to speak to Dawn whether you come with me or not."

Elisabeth looked at her helplessly. She couldn't let Mariella go in there alone, asking questions about Tomas, but everything in her was screaming that this was a bad idea.

"I've been to the club before and know the bouncers. We can get in quickly," Mariella said. "We'll chat with my cousin, and be out in half an hour."

Elisabeth and Liam exchanged uneasy glances. This was their best lead. And they couldn't let Mariella go in alone.

"All right," Elisabeth said. "We're going to Sayawan tonight."

Elisabeth stared in amazement at the miniature radio transmitter attached to a tiny microphone that Liam held out to her. "A wire? How did you get that?"

Liam shrugged. "I made a few phone calls while you and Mariella were getting dolled up."

She put her hands on her hips. "You went out alone, with the Bagsics all aware you're in L.A.?"

"It was only for a few minutes, and I met with people I trust." Liam shoved the wire at her again. "Use the medical tape to attach this to your skin, under your shirt. That way, I can listen in. If things go south, I can try to get into the club to help." His mouth was tight, and a muscle was working in his jaw. He clearly wasn't happy about this entire situation, and Elisabeth figured the wire was his way of having some feeling of control.

"That's a good idea." Mariella drew Elisabeth toward the bathroom in her apartment. "Let's put that on you."

Once they were inside the bathroom, Elisabeth untied the brocade corset she wore over a long-sleeved shirt with ruffled cuffs, both borrowed from Mariella. They had both chosen gothic-themed clothes, which enabled them to wear extraheavy makeup. Mariella wore a black leather jacket over a skirt and knee-length boots.

"He's just worried for you," Mariella said as she attached the wire.

"I know." It was strange to have someone worrying about her. She was so used to people not caring about her at all. But over the past couple days, she'd come to appreciate Liam, and to draw comfort in knowing he had her back.

"There," Mariella said. "You're wired for sound."

"Let's go." She marched out into Mariella's living room where Liam was waiting.

They'd held off until later in the evening so their arrival would be less noticeable. Liam parked near the back door, then got out the headphones attached to the receiver for the wire Elisabeth wore. "Let's do a sound check."

She reached behind her and turned on the radio transmitter. "Testing."

He nodded. "I can hear you fine." He held her gaze, his mouth set in a firm, unhappy line. "Be careful."

She forced herself to break eye contact and aimed for a light tone of voice. "I will."

Sayawan announced its presence with a huge neon sign above what looked to be a former manufacturing plant. The driving beat of dance music was muted in the darkness. Lights strung along the eaves all around the building showed clusters of men waiting in line. Women ambled to the front double glass doors, where the bouncers usually let them inside immediately.

"Here we go," Mariella muttered, and led the way to the front doors. She smiled up at the bouncer. Elisabeth tossed her hair in its new pixie cut and added her smile.

The bouncer barely glanced at them before opening the doors for them. "Thanks," Mariella chirped as they went inside.

The volume of the music hit Elisabeth like a door to the face. Liam wouldn't be able to hear anything through the wire. Come to think of it, *she* wouldn't be able to hear anything if she tried to speak to Dawn.

"Come on," Mariella shouted. "It's quieter near the bar."

They navigated around the edges of the large room, illuminated only by brightly colored lights from the DJ box high up on the far wall balcony. The huge dance floor was packed with people, and even more clustered around the scattered bistro tables and up on the balcony that ran along three of the walls.

Elisabeth noticed several people with small plastic bags in their hands. They had a sticker with an image of a blue sun with sword blades for rays, similar to the symbol on the Filipino flag. The bags had small amounts of what looked like cherry-red–colored rock salt.

Crystal meth. She was almost sure of it. From the amount she could see, she would guess that this club was a hub for the Bagsics' drug trade.

The bar was off to the side of the main room, set back into the wall and shielded from the dance floor by a two-story-high pile of wooden crates erected as decor art. To the side of the bar was a set of swinging double doors leading to the kitchen.

Mariella snagged a bistro table in a corner, and they only had to wait a few minutes before she waved frantically to one of the waitresses, a petite girl with a long braid whose face lit up when she saw Mariella. She finished serving food to a table, then wove between the chairs to their table. "Hey, cuz! This isn't your usual night to come here."

"Dawn, I brought a friend, Elisabeth." Mariella leaned closer and Elisabeth could only just hear it as she said, "She's the one who helped Joslyn get away from Tomas."

Dawn's face paled, but she anxiously asked Elisabeth, "Is Joslyn okay?"

"As far as I know."

"Tomas will never stop looking for her," Mariella said.

"I'm trying to find proof that Tomas killed Joslyn's father," Elisabeth said. "The only way Joslyn will be safe will be if Tomas is behind bars. Did you know that his alibi was that he was here that night?"

Dawn shook her head, then bit her lip, and her eyes skated around the room briefly.

"I'm not a cop," Elisabeth said. "Would you be willing to tell me about the night of the murder?"

"They'd kill me if they knew I was talking to you about that," Dawn said in a low voice.

Elisabeth touched the girl's hand briefly. "They will never find out from me or Mariella."

"It's for Joslyn," Mariella said to her cousin. "You know what Tomas did to her, and then he killed her father. We can't let him get away with that."

Dawn's eyes were still troubled, but her chin firmed.

"Did you see Tomas here the night of the murder?" Elisabeth asked.

"Yes, but he didn't come here until just before closing at three."

Elisabeth's hands clenched in her lap. She knew he couldn't have been here, but hearing confirmation was more important to her than she'd expected. "What did he look like?"

"He was really agitated. Worried, but angry at the same time."

"Did you notice any blood on his clothes?"

Dawn bit her lip again. "I thought there were some dark stains on his cuffs, but the club is dark, and his clothes that night were dark, too, so I can't be sure."

"What did he do? Who did he talk to?"

"He talked to one of the big bosses." Dawn glanced around. "I don't see the man here tonight. They spoke in Filipino, so I didn't understand what they were saying to each other, but when the boss got on his cell phone, I heard him say the name Terence. People say that he's their…cleaner."

Elisabeth felt a chill along the base of her spine. They sent a cleaner to the crime scene? He would have erased any evidence that led back to Tomas. "If you told the police what you saw—"

"No!" Dawn shook her head frantically. "No way. I won't testify against a Bagsic."

"But—"

"A few years ago, someone else testified against a Bagsic," Mariella said. "The Bagsic got off on a technicality, and the witness and his entire family were killed."

Elisabeth shivered. She told Dawn, "I wouldn't ask you to make yourself or your family a target."

But they needed concrete evidence. There had to be something, someone they could pursue who could give them what they needed to have Tomas arrested and convicted. "Dawn, who was with Tomas that night?"

"Two other captains in the gang. They call one of them Shades because he's into sunglasses. I don't know his real name and I only know the other guy by sight." Dawn glanced around. "Actually, they're here tonight. That's them over there." She pointed to two men sitting several tables away.

At just that moment, one of the men looked up and saw Dawn gesturing to them, and the three women looking at them. A slimy smile spread across his thin lips.

"Oh, no." Dawn turned back to Elisabeth and Mariella, her eyes wide.

"Go," Elisabeth told her.

As Dawn scurried away, she looked back to the man. He nudged his friend, said something to him without taking his eyes off of the women and then the two of them got up and started walking toward Elisabeth's table.

"What will we do?" Mariella hissed.

"Follow my lead." Elisabeth affected a casual pose, forcing her rigid shoulders to relax. She stared directly at the two men, her mouth pulled into what she hoped was a coy smile.

The men came up to their table, one of them leaning his elbow heavily against it. "Hey, ladies." He was swaying, even with the support of the table, and Elisabeth caught the strong smell of alcohol on his breath.

"Hi." Elisabeth leaned her elbow against the table, too, mirroring his gestures.

"I'm Manny. This is Shades." He nodded toward the other man, who wasn't wearing sunglasses indoors but did have an expensive pair tucked into the pocket of his purple Armani shirt. Manny blinked at her blankly for a moment, and Elisabeth wondered for a second if he was drunk enough to pass out in front of them, but then he said, "So you're friends with Dawn?"

"Oh, sure," Elisabeth said. "But I know Tomas better."

"Tomas?" Manny's dark eyebrows rose. "Baby, don't you know he's already taken? But I'm free." He gave a loose-lipped smile and leaned closer to her.

Elisabeth faked a pout. "He didn't seem taken the last

time I saw him. You guys are friends, right? What'll happen if he sees me talking to you?" She gave him a bold look from beneath lowered eyelids.

Manny's wide smile glinted brightly in the darkness of the club. "Oh, trust me, we learned to share when we were in kindergarten."

Elisabeth had to fight to suppress a shudder. "Where is Tomas anyway?" she asked. "I haven't seen him in a few days."

"He's up in Northern California somewhere."

Manny either hadn't been told exactly where, or maybe he hadn't cared. Either way, perhaps Tomas's business in Sonoma wasn't widely known. "Northern California?" Elisabeth pretended to look disdainful that anyone would choose to travel up there. "Why?"

Manny shrugged, then he caught sight of another gang member walking past and called to him. He said in Tagalog, "Hey, Alfonso, do you know why Tomas is up north?"

"Naw," Alfonso replied, also in Tagalog. "No one knows except the bosses."

"It might be better for him to stay up there," Shades said with a sneer. "Especially after he lost that shipping container off the *Pansit*."

What shipping container?

Unaware that Elisabeth had understood them, Manny turned to her and said in English, "He'll be gone for a while, baby. How about you play with me instead?"

Shades had been giving Mariella appraising looks from beneath his heavy brows, but she'd kept her gaze on the table. Elisabeth could feel her knee shaking where it touched hers under the table.

Elisabeth said to Manny, "I wish I could, but I have to take my friend home. She's not feeling so hot."

Shades's mouth curled in disgust and he leaned back slightly. Then he said to Manny in Tagalog, "I'm outta here." Without bothering to say anything to the women, he turned and followed where Alfonso had gone, deeper into the club.

Well, that took care of him. Elisabeth had been afraid she'd need to resort to more creative measures to get rid of him.

"I can take you both home." Manny fumbled in his suit jacket pocket a few times before pulling out a ring of keys and jingling them in front of her.

As if she'd get anywhere near a car with him. Even without his smarmy manner, his blood alcohol level must be through the roof. But she jumped to her feet with alacrity. "Oh, sure. Let's go."

Mariella gave her a wild-eyed look. Elisabeth returned it with a calculating expression of her own, hoping Mariella got the message.

Manny clamped onto her elbow with a large, heavy hand, but he was staggering dangerously. "Let's go out the back door," she said through a puff of breath as he stumbled and dragged down on her arm.

Once they'd exited, Elisabeth cast a glance around to make sure there wasn't anyone else around, then prepared to throw a carefully aimed blow that would knock the drunken man out.

But before she could do it, a shadow separated from behind a Dumpster and rushed toward them. She barely had time to recognize Liam before he tackled Manny to the ground.

Liam's attack must have shot adrenaline through Manny's system, temporarily shoving aside the fog of his drunkenness, because he began throwing heavy, powerful punches.

But Liam was more fit and agile, plus he was sober. He dodged the clumsy blows and rammed his elbow against Manny's head. The gang member went limp.

Elisabeth found she was breathing heavily, almost as if she'd been the one in the fight. "Are you all ri—"

"What were you thinking, bringing him out here?" Liam got to his feet, his eyes boring into hers.

She glared at him. "I was thinking that I'd knock him out."

"He's twice your weight. He could have killed you."

She thrust a hand toward Manny's inert form. "He was drunk enough that he'd have been out like a light from just a tap."

"Of all the foolhardy…" Liam pressed his lips together, and a vein throbbed in his temple. "You were taking a big risk."

The last man who had yelled at her had been her ex-boyfriend, Cruise, who'd punctuated his anger with insults and his fists on her face. She knew Liam wasn't Cruise, but the way he yelled at her made her hurt deep down. And that, in turn, made her lash out.

"I have been taking care of myself since I was sixteen. I never asked you for your help!"

"Guys!" Mariella's voice cut through the haze of rage in front of her eyes.

Elisabeth blinked, and realized Mariella had shouted at them several times.

"We need to go," Mariella said urgently. "Before your yelling catches someone's attention."

Elisabeth felt as if her head was still steaming. She stalked past Liam and headed toward her car, ripping the microphone and taped wire from her torso as she walked. She unhooked them from the radio transmitter and tossed them all into the glove compartment. Mariella climbed into the backseat and Liam started the car, all in silence.

As they drove away, Elisabeth heard her words again as clearly as if they were played back into her ears. She had worked so hard not to be vulnerable, ever, but Liam got to her. In that way, he was more dangerous to her than Tomas.

There was a buzzing sound, and Liam pulled his cell phone from his pocket. Fumbling his Bluetooth headset into place, he answered the call. "Hey, Shaun." His tone was clipped, but Elisabeth wasn't sure if it was because of the caller or because he was still mad at her.

His brow wrinkled. "Why?" Then shock washed over his face. "I'm…I'm in L.A. I'll be there as soon as possible." He disconnected the call. "We have to go back to Sonoma." His voice skated the edge of panic.

"What's wrong?"

"That was my brother. He said he stopped two men who tried to break into my father's house tonight." Liam's eyes were wide as she glanced at her. "I think one of them was Tomas."

EIGHT

He'd put his family in danger. The guilt lay heavy in his stomach, a seething, pulsing tumor. He'd already put Elisabeth and Joslyn in danger. Now his father and brothers were at risk, too.

How could he fix this? He had to make things right.

They'd dropped Mariella off at her apartment in Los Angeles, receiving only a halfhearted agreement not to put herself in danger in investigating Tomas further. Liam didn't quite believe her, but he'd been too anxious to start the return drive to Sonoma to stay and argue.

Elisabeth had sat silent for most of the six-hour drive. She'd scrubbed the makeup from her face and given Mariella back the clothes she'd borrowed, but she looked very different with her new short haircut, coupled with the lighter color. She'd withdrawn into herself ever since they'd argued in the parking lot of the club.

Listening to what he could hear of her conversations while she was in the club had been excruciating for Liam. He hadn't been able to help her, to do anything to back her up in that dangerous situation. When she hadn't been able to get rid of Manny's company, he'd grasped on to the idea that he could get the guy away from her once she got him outside the club. And so he'd tackled the slimeball with all the force of his pent-up frustration.

But then he'd lashed out at her, because she'd spent half an hour driving him crazy. It hadn't really been her fault, it had been the situation, but he hadn't been able to distinguish it in his mind at the moment.

And she'd looked at him with loathing. That had cut him as deeply as the war wound in his shoulder.

During the drive, after he'd calmed down, he'd tried twice to apologize, but she cut him off both times by saying, "I don't want to talk about it."

He hadn't tried a third time.

She drove for part of the way so he could sleep, and then he'd taken over. She'd been sleeping for the past several hours, her head resting against the closed window. In sleep, her face had lost its toughness, showing a soft vulnerability in her lips and cheeks.

He didn't want to be attracted to her. He didn't want to care about her. But something about her made him feel more whole than he'd felt since returning from Afghanistan.

But the reality was that he was horribly broken, and he should keep his distance from this woman. She had her own problems, her own cares, her own baggage. He couldn't put his burdens on her.

Just as he had been trying not to put his burdens on his family. And yet, danger had found them anyway. There must be something he could do to stop this, to make this situation all right again.

He took a back-way shortcut to his father's house, cutting through some access roads, and finally turned onto the long dirt road between vineyards that led to his father's eight-acre lot. The sun played hide-and-seek behind the clouds. The changing light made the day vacillate between gloomy and cheerful.

Finally the road ended before the two-story house. The front door was on the second story, and behind, the land sloped downward, with a magnificent view of the rolling farmlands, lined with grapevines, and a distant mountain. The effect of the professionally landscaped front yard was ruined by the strings of Christmas lights on everything green. Shaun had also erected some lit reindeer figures and decorated the tallest tree with gigantic gold, red and green ornament balls.

"We're here." Liam parked along the side of the driveway and cut the engine.

Elisabeth stretched and yawned. "What time is it?"

"Almost seven."

Despite the early hour, the front door opened and Liam's eldest brother, Shaun, headed toward them, followed by his wife, Monica. They must have been in the front room watching for them.

"You made good time, Liam." Monica launched herself at him, holding him in a hug that soothed the ragged edges of his worry. As a former nurse, Monica had a way about her that made him feel as if he'd just stepped into a safe haven.

"How's Dad?" Liam asked.

"He's fine." Despite the reassuring words, Shaun's forehead was creased in a frown.

"How're you?" Liam tried to make his voice casual, but Shaun's piercing blue eyes saw right through him.

A smile creased his brother's rugged face. "Better now that you're here." He then folded Liam into a bone-creaking hug, as if completely aware that it would embarrass him in front of Elisabeth.

But when Liam emerged from his brother's harder-than-normal back slapping, he was surprised at the expression on Elisabeth's face. Rather than humor, she seemed startled, and there was a hollowness to her eyes, almost like… envy. But that was silly. He was probably just tired and seeing things.

"Elisabeth, this is my brother Shaun and his wife, Monica."

"Come inside, it's chilly out here." Monica put a gentle arm around Elisabeth to guide her into the house, and Liam was a bit surprised to see his capable, fiercely independent partner docilely submit to his sister-in-law.

Shaun put a hand on his shoulder to hold him back for a moment. "Dad knows about the attempted break-in, but I haven't told him anything about the Bagsics or that you were down in L.A. six hours ago."

Liam's father was sitting in a recliner in the living room at the back of the house. A cheerful fire burned in the stone fireplace that dominated the room, and the scent of pine filled the air from the garlands strung along the mantel.

"Dad, I thought you'd still be lazing around in bed." Liam grinned at his father as he clapped a hand on his shoulder. Dad's bones seemed more prominent than they'd been only a couple weeks ago.

"I got up early to keep Shaun company. After what happened last night, your brother was too scared to go back to sleep." His father's blue eyes, exactly like Shaun's, twinkled up at him.

Shaun rolled his eyes. "As if. I was making sure Dad didn't go storming outside with his shotgun."

"If it had been me last night, I'd have hit more than just the kumquat tree."

Monica gave her husband a whack on the arm. "You hit my kumquat tree? When were you going to tell me?"

Shaun tried to look innocent. "I just did?"

She glared at him and crossed her arms in front of her, although a smile peeked out at the corner of her mouth. "You did that on purpose."

"What?" Shaun held out his hands. "I'm not that good a shot."

"You're a terrible shot. But you only needed to fire in the general direction to take out my kumquat tree."

"Why would he want to take out your kumquat tree?" Elisabeth looked bewildered and amused at the same time.

"Because Shaun detests kumquats."

"It's Liam's fault." Shaun pointed a finger.

"I was only six." Liam laughed, taking a step back. "You were a whopping twelve, old enough to know better."

Monica said to Elisabeth, "Supposedly Shaun had a kumquat-eating contest with Liam and won. By a long shot."

"And then got very sick all over my Foreman grill," his dad added.

And then Elisabeth laughed.

Liam hadn't seen her laugh before. Her eyes turned into chips of amber, and joy radiated from her like the sun rising above the horizon. She even gave a little snort before she got her breath back.

His dad said to Shaun, "Go get us some coffee. I can't talk about you behind your back while you're still here."

"Yes, sir." Shaun turned to go.

"Ooh, I've got a good one about Liam," Monica said to Elisabeth.

"And that's my cue." Liam went after Shaun.

In the kitchen, Liam leaned against the granite countertop while Shaun put on the coffeemaker. "So what happened last night?"

"It sounds more dramatic than it really was. Monica was supposed to check Dad's blood pressure, so she was in Dad's bedroom with the lights out, working on her laptop, when around two, the motion-sensing floodlights in the backyard came on. At first she didn't think much of it because we saw a coyote come close to the house last week, but she happened to glance outside when the lights came on, and she saw a human-shaped shadow moving behind the trees, toward the house."

Liam felt as if a fist squeezed his heart. What if his sister-in-law hadn't been awake? What if Monica hadn't happened to look out and see the shadow?

"She woke me up immediately. I went to the living room and hid behind the curtains," Shaun said. "I saw two men approach the side door—dressed in black, dark hair, average build. She dialed 9-1-1 while I got the shotguns out of the gun cabinet and called out for them to get off my property. Monica and I both pumped our shotguns—they were only loaded with rock salt, but you know the sound of shotguns being primed is pretty intimidating. We could see out the window when they ran away."

Liam ran his hand down his face. "I just thank God you all are okay."

"They looked like just two random thieves, but Nathan told me about the Bagsics, so I wondered. But I'm afraid I didn't get a good enough look at them to know if they were Filipino, or wearing purple and gray or not."

"How did Dad take it?"

"Oh, you know Dad. He said that if he'd had the shotgun, he'd have peppered their backsides with rock salt just to teach them a lesson."

Liam smiled briefly, then sighed. "I'm sorry about all this. The Bagsics wouldn't have come here if not for me."

"Hey." Shaun clapped a hand on Liam's shoulder, his grip tight. "This isn't your fault. Besides, we still don't know for sure if this was the gang."

"But if it is, they're not going away. I have to make sure you're all safe."

"*We'll* make sure we're all safe. You, me and God."

Liam looked away. "Faith has been hard for me lately."

"I understand. I've had to learn the hard way to trust God."

Liam had noticed that since he'd started dating Monica, Shaun had been more sure in his faith, and stronger somehow in his personality. It was something Liam envied, because he'd felt so weak lately. He wanted strength to heal himself.

But he didn't have time right now. He needed to keep his family safe, at least until he found evidence to put Tomas in jail.

One of their brothers, Michael, was still overseas with his job, but their brother Brady and his wife and son were in Geyserville, north of Sonoma. "Do you think the gang would know where to find Brady?"

Grave lines carved alongside Shaun's mouth. "I'm not sure."

Liam had an idea. "Brady and his family should move in here, too." Shaun was head of security at the Joy Luck Life Hotel and Spa as well as a former border patrol officer. If everyone was under one roof, he'd be able to keep them safe.

Shaun's eyebrows shot up. "He's not going to like that."

"He just had a son. He'll want to protect him."

"I should have rephrased. *Debra's* not going to like that."

Liam rubbed the back of his neck. He and Brady's wife didn't get along. Early in their marriage, Debra had been almost smothering in her attempts to integrate with the O'Neill family, but later, she'd gotten cooler in her attitude—toward them and toward her husband. Liam thought Debra didn't treat Brady very well sometimes and he had been tactless enough to tell her once, in private. She'd gotten upset and told Brady.

If Liam came to her with some crazy idea about moving into her father-in-law's home, she might refuse just to spite Liam.

"I have to try," Liam said. "I can't keep investigating Tomas until I know you're all safe from the Bagsics."

Shaun cast an eye on the clock hanging on the wall. "Well, if you're going to talk to them both, you should go now, so you can catch him before he leaves for work."

Monica insisted they wait while she packed bagels and cream cheese for their breakfast, but within minutes Liam and Elisabeth had left, driving north toward Geyserville. Liam called Brady to let him know they were coming.

"Hey, Liam, what's up?" Brady's words were friendly but there was a dullness to his tone. Liam wondered if he was still upset at what Liam had said to Debra.

"I need to talk to both you and Debra. Will you still be home in half an hour?"

Brady gave a deep sigh. "I need to go to work, Liam."

He had never been reluctant to talk to Liam before. "You own your own business, Brady, you can go in anytime. This is important."

"Okay. We'll be here." He disconnected the call.

"I've been thinking about what we should do after we talk to your brother," Elisabeth said. "We need to find out more information about that shipping container that Tomas lost." Despite her cool attitude toward him on the drive to Sonoma, she had shared the information she'd overheard the Bagsics discussing in Filipino.

"I also want to ask Nathan Fischer to talk to his LAPD contacts about Tomas's two friends, Shades and Manny."

"That's a good idea." A hint of warmth crept back into her tone.

"I'm wondering if we can find evidence on one of them for the murder. They might be willing to flip on Tomas."

"Evidence won't be easy to find if a cleaner went through the murder scene."

Liam shrugged. "No one's perfect. That includes cleaners."

Brady and his wife had bought a nice five-acre lot just off the highway in Geyserville and built a pretty, Spanish-style home. Their driveway wound up toward the house for a quarter mile, bordered by trees and shrubs. Their only Christmas decoration was an expensive-looking wreath on the front door.

Debra answered their knock, orange-colored baby food smeared on her cheek and glopped in her hair. Her scowl at Liam quickly morphed into pleasant politeness at the sight of Elisabeth. "Liam, I didn't know you were bringing a guest." There was a slight bite to her words.

"Sorry, I forgot to mention Elisabeth when I called Brady. Elisabeth Aday, meet Debra O'Neill."

"Nice to meet you," Elisabeth said quietly.

Brady appeared behind her, holding his baby son. "Did you have breakfast?"

Debra's mouth tightened at his words, and Liam was grateful for Monica's bagels that they'd eaten during the drive as he said, "Yes."

"Come on in."

"I need to clean up." Debra turned and headed down the hallway to the bathroom, leaving Brady with Liam and Elisabeth.

"This way." He nodded toward the living room, just to the side of the entrance foyer.

"We're sorry to interrupt you in the middle of break-fast." Brady's living room was out of a home fashion magazine, even down to the Christmas tree in the corner decorated with color-coordinated silver and white ribbons and ball ornaments. Liam hated it. He sat gingerly in a snow-white leather couch in front of the glass coffee table. Elisabeth perched on the edge of a white-and-gray-striped silk chair.

"It takes twice as long now with Ryan, here." Brady relaxed into a dove-gray leather recliner. His son regarded them with wide blue eyes. "What did you need to talk about?"

Liam shifted uncomfortably in his seat. "I'm afraid I've put you and your family in danger."

Brady's brows lowered over his bright blue eyes, and in that moment, he looked exactly like Shaun. "What kind of danger? Are you okay?"

"It's actually because of me." Elisabeth's voice was low, calm, and it seemed to help ease some of the stiffness out of Brady's shoulders. "I work as a private investigator and also volunteer at a women's shelter. Recently, I helped a woman escape her ex-boyfriend, unaware that he was a captain in a Filipino gang. The gang came after me and Liam got caught in the middle. Since the gang knows Liam is helping me, they might be targeting Liam's family, also."

Brady shook his head. "That seems far-fetched. This isn't the movies. They're not going to torture us for information about Liam."

"Dad's house was attacked last night," Liam blurted out.

Brady paled. "Is he all right? What happened?"

"Shaun scared off the intruders before they could get inside."

"And you're sure that the intruders were part of this gang?"

"Well…no," Liam admitted. "But it seems likely."

"Filipino culture puts a lot of emphasis on the family unit," Elisabeth said. "The threat to a person's family is intended as a personal insult. That's why the gang would target you."

"We have a good security system, and I'll be careful—"

"Brady, it might be safer for Debra and Ryan if you moved to Dad's house for a little while."

"Absolutely not." Debra's voice cut into the living room from where she stood in the open doorway. She propped her hands on her hips. "Why do you want us to move?"

Liam explained to her, but Debra only shook her head more vigorously. "That's ridiculous. You don't even know for certain if the men were gang members. This 'threat' might be all in your head, Liam."

Brady's eyes were hard as he regarded his wife. "Liam doesn't exaggerate or make things up."

The look Debra cast Brady was almost disdainful. "I was simply saying that he could be mistaken."

"You don't think it would be better to be safe than sorry?" Elisabeth said. "Think of what's best for your baby. These men are very dangerous."

"You'd only need to stay with Dad for a little while," Liam said.

"It's Christmas." Debra's voice was sharp. "I'm not packing everything up to go to Patrick's house just because you have a funny feeling." Debra's derisive tone included both Liam and Brady.

Liam wasn't sure what was going on between Brady and his wife, but it was obvious Debra still held a grudge against him for what he'd said to her. But despite her feelings toward him, he couldn't leave them unprotected like this. "How about if we stay with the two of you?" Liam said.

Debra's brows drew down over her eyes and she opened her mouth to say something, but Brady spoke first. "You're always welcome to stay with us, Liam." He cast a brief, hard look at his wife, who closed her mouth and gave a small sniff.

"Just for a little while," Liam said. "Just in case there is a threat."

Brady smiled at him. "Between my work and yours, we never get to hang out anymore."

As kids, Liam had been closest to Brady. They both enjoyed computers, science fiction and *Star Trek*. But Brady's marriage and Liam's deployment had caused them to drift apart. Maybe now that he was back in Sonoma, Liam could rebuild that relationship.

Liam stood. "We need to go talk to Nathan, and then we'll be back."

Debra gave a sigh that skated the edge of long suffering. "I'll get the guest rooms ready for you two."

Elisabeth also stood, her eyes neutral as they rested on Debra's retreating back. But she smiled at Brady. "Thanks for letting us stay."

"I'll walk you out to your car." Ryan was sleepily resting against his father's shoulder, and he only stirred a little as Brady rose and headed out the front door with them.

Elisabeth cast Liam and Brady only a brief glance before she said, "I'll wait in the car." And then she left them alone on the front stoop.

A brief silence fell between them. Liam looked back at the closed front door and sobered. "Brady, is everything okay with Debra?"

Brady's eyes became chips of blue ice. "Everything's fine," he said in a clipped voice.

"Brady…"

"It's between me and my wife. I'm not talking about this with you, Liam."

He could respect that. "It's not a problem for us to stay here?"

Brady's mouth softened. "It's never a problem to spend time with you, bro."

Liam kissed his nephew's soft hair, then clasped Brady's shoulder in a warm grip. "We'll be back in a few."

As he headed toward the car, he saw Elisabeth's eyes on him. There was a strange expression on her face as she regarded him, then Brady. Bleakness flashed over her face, then was gone.

He got into the passenger seat just as her phone rang.

She frowned as she saw the caller ID. "That's the number for the shelter. Hello?"

Her perplexed expression melted to worry. "Are you sure?" she breathed.

"What is it?" Liam leaned closer to her.

"O-okay. Thanks." She disconnected the call, then turned to him. "It was the shelter. They said that Joslyn called them."

NINE

Elisabeth stared at her cell phone. Everything in her wanted to help Joslyn, and yet…too much didn't add up.

"What did she say?" Liam looked as flabbergasted as she felt.

"According to Kalea, Joslyn said that she spotted Tomas and needed my help. Then she hung up."

Liam's eyes narrowed. "She didn't say where she was?"

"No. And she knows I don't know where she is. We were in the process of figuring out where she should go, but she left the shelter before we finalized any plans." Elisabeth hefted her cell phone in her hand. "And why did she call the shelter?"

"Does she have your cell phone number?"

"I change it pretty often, but I have an answering service that I check regularly. That's the number I give my clients."

"She might have forgotten the number." But even as he said it, Liam looked suspicious.

"That's possible…"

"Or it's a trick by the Bagsics to get you to find Joslyn and lead them to her."

That had been her second thought. Her first had been concern and worry for Joslyn, if Tomas really had found her.

Liam took her cell phone from her hand. His touch was

light, but she felt calluses on his fingertips where they brushed against her palm. "If it's really Joslyn, she'll call the shelter again," he said.

"I know you're right, but—" she swallowed "—I'm worried about her."

"We'll bring Tomas to justice, and then Joslyn won't have to run anymore."

His confidence made her feel steadier. He seemed to always have that effect on her. She didn't understand why.

And she didn't want to get used to relying on it—or him.

She started the engine. "Where to?"

"Back to Sonoma, to Nathan's house."

Elisabeth glanced at the gas gauge. Her old car didn't have great gas mileage, and her tank was low. "I need to stop at a gas station."

"There's one on the way to Highway 101, off a side road."

It was a short drive to the gas station. She was about to swipe her credit card at the pump when a fast-moving figure caught her attention. She turned around to see a Filipino man leaning on the passenger-side window, which was open, saying something to Liam in a low voice she couldn't catch.

Her heart blipped, and she was about to head toward them when a man's voice sounded in her ear. "Don't move." A hard object was shoved into her ribs.

He was close enough that she could smell cigarettes and a spicy, flamboyant cologne. She turned her head and saw a Filipino man next to her, his face familiar, his dark eyes hard as flint.

"Walk." He punctuated the command with a jab of the gun held against her side. "Toward the back of the station."

She walked, every movement stiff. She looked around to see if anyone had noticed them, but no one was looking their way. She could shout to the convenience store attendant, but that might get her—or worse, the attendant—shot. Or Liam.

She turned the corner toward the back of the building and spotted the SUV parked there. It was the same one from the parking lot of her apartment building, with the fancy scrollwork detail along the side.

These weren't Bagsics.

"How did you find us?" She tried to sound frightened, to make the man let down his guard.

"I didn't think your boyfriend would visit his brother way out here, but the boss said to scope out the house anyway. Wait'll I deliver you to them." There was a nasty smile in his voice.

Who were these guys? They obviously had bad blood with the Bagsics. Hoping a taunt would trick him into sharing some information, she said, "You Bagsics are all alike."

The man recoiled in disgust. "We're Tumibays, not Bagsic scum."

She hadn't heard of them, but they must be a gang. The man was dressed in a black T-shirt and leather jacket, with scuffed jeans and boots. She could see tattoos on his wrists where his jacket cuffs had ridden up.

At that moment, the second gang member appeared from around the corner with Liam, whose face was a thundercloud. But his eyes quickly found hers. "Are you all right?"

She nodded.

Liam's hands curled into fists. "Okay, you got us. Now, what do you want?"

The man with the leather jacket studied Elisabeth. She noticed a pale, almost invisible scar along his left cheekbone in the shape of a large fishing hook.

"We figured Tomas would come looking for his girlfriend," the man said, "but what does he want with you?"

Elisabeth had to fight to prevent the shock from appearing on her face. What exactly did they know? "How do you know about Tomas and Joslyn?"

"Oh, us and Joslyn are old friends." The man had a smile on his face that made her shudder. Joslyn was involved with the Tumibays?

Liam's eyes narrowed. "If that's true, then you know where she is, right? She'd hide out with her 'old friends.'"

The man's smile grew hard. "I'm not going to ask you again. Why are the Bagsics after you?" The barely leashed violence in his stance made it clear that if she didn't answer, he was ready and willing to resort to violence.

Elisabeth clamped her mouth shut, fighting back the dark memories in her mind. He needed information from them, so he probably wouldn't shoot her, but he might hit her. She couldn't afford to flash back to her ex-boyfriend, to the blows she'd received at his hand. She had to keep it together.

The man regarded her curiously. "You know about Joslyn. So that must mean Tomas wants you because you know something about her. Maybe where she is."

"Or they know about the shipping container," the other man said.

"Shut up, moron," the first man hissed.

The shipping container that Tomas had somehow lost? How were the Tumibays involved in that? And did Joslyn have something to do with it?

"Who cares why the Bagsics are after us? What do you want?" Elisabeth tried to make her voice tremble in fear, but she thought she might have sounded too belligerent.

"We want whatever Tomas wants from you. Give it to us and we'll let you go." She didn't believe him for a second. If he got what he was after, he'd either kill them or take them back to their gang bosses.

She needed to separate these two, because that was the only way she and Liam could disarm them. "It's on my laptop, in the car." She cast her eyes downward in an expression of defeat.

"What are you doing? Don't give them anything," Liam said. She hadn't expected him to play along with her, but she was glad he was. It made the gang member even more eager to get her laptop.

"Let's go." The man came up next to her, his arm around her waist so he could hide his gun against her side.

"Liam…" She looked up at him. He was standing stiffly in front of the other man, who had his own gun trained on him.

"He'll stay here, safe and sound," the gang member said.

As she walked to her car, she was more aware than ever of the smell of oil and gasoline. What was she thinking, taking on a guy with a gun in the middle of a gas station?

But this was still her best chance for getting away—now, when there were only two of them. If Liam and Elisabeth were taken back to their bosses, there would be more gang members, and no hope of escape.

She looked again at the gas station attendant, but he was reading a magazine. Even if he looked up, he would only see the gang member with his arm around Elisabeth.

The gang member released her so she could take out her laptop case. She turned to hand it to him, but deliberately held it directly in front of his gun. He automatically shifted the gun to the side.

She released her grip on the laptop case handle at the same time that her other hand struck out at his gun hand, forcing the weapon to fly several yards away. She followed up with a sharp jab to his neck that made him cough and double over.

The laptop dropped to the ground. She flung a punch toward the man's lowered head, but he ducked and she only grazed his ear. The man grabbed at her, throwing her to the ground.

The cement smacked into her back, forcing air out of her lungs in a sharp "Oof!" The man took advantage and straddled her, trying to restrain her.

Before he could get a solid guard stance, she lifted her hips and flung him sideways, rolling with him and grabbing at his arm. She used her hips as a fulcrum and pulled at his wrist, applying a jujitsu arm bar.

He shouted in pain and yanked at his arm to pull it out of her grip, and she felt one of the bones in his forearm snap. She released him immediately. He rolled over, grabbing his arm, shouting obscenities at her.

"Hey!" The gas station attendant had finally seen them, alerted by the man's shouts, and he charged out of the building. "I've called the police!"

The gang member got up and ran toward his SUV. Elisabeth followed on shaky knees. She had to help Liam.

She turned the corner in time to see Liam landing punches to the man's torso. Elisabeth's attacker ran past them, jumping into the truck and cranking the engine.

Liam's attacker, hearing the truck, shoved hard at Liam. It made him stagger backward right into Elisabeth, and they fell in a tangle of limbs.

The truck jammed out of the gas station with a roar of the engine.

Liam rolled over and grabbed her shoulders. "Are you all right?"

"I'm fine. What happened to his—"

"What were you thinking?" His blue eyes were wild as they bored into hers.

She pushed at him. "Why are you always yelling at me?"

He rolled onto his back and closed his eyes, breathing heavily. "I'm sorry. I was yelling at you because you took ten years off my life. I was worried for you."

Who was the last person who had worried about her?

Not her father, not her ex-boyfriend. No one since her mother had died, since she was sixteen.

"I knew you'd be able to take that guy out if you had him alone," she mumbled. She slowly got to her feet.

The attendant turned the corner. "Are you guys okay?"

Elisabeth waved to him. The adrenaline rush made her arms and legs shake uncontrollably, and she leaned against the side of the building for support.

"The police should be here soon," the attendant said.

"Where's the guy's gun?" Elisabeth asked Liam.

"Gun?" The attendant's eyes goggled.

Liam pointed to the bushes behind the building. "I'll call Detective Carter to let him know what happened."

Elisabeth pushed away from the building to go look for her attacker's weapon so the police could take it when they arrived. She found the gun, and the sight of it lying on the concrete made her remember fighting the man, fighting for her life.

He hadn't been a Bagsic. He'd been a Tumibay, an entirely different Filipino gang.

There were not one, but *two* gangs after them.

The Geyserville police showed up within a few minutes, and half an hour later, Elisabeth saw Detective Carter's car appear. He spoke to the Geyserville officers, then came up to Liam and Elisabeth. "You guys are going to qualify for frequent customer points."

Liam gave a weak smile, then grimaced. Bruises were starting to show up on his face from where the gang member had gotten some punches in. Elisabeth wanted to grimace, too, at the pain he must be feeling.

Detective Carter's face grew grave. "Was it the Bagsics or the Tumibays?"

Elisabeth blinked at him. "Tumibays. How did you know about them?"

"We looked at traffic cameras around your apartment after the Bagsics attacked you and noted the license plate for the SUV with scrollwork along the sides. When I found out about this attack, I was just about to call you to ask you to come to the station to look at this." Detective Carter showed them a driver's license photo of a Filipino man with a fishhook-shaped scar on his face. His name was visible—Lamar Garcia.

"That's one of the guys who attacked us here," Liam said, "although I can't say for certain I remember seeing him outside Elisabeth's apartment."

Elisabeth nodded agreement. "We only got a glimpse of them. Who is he?"

Detective Carter sighed. "He's known to be one of the Tumibays."

"What can you tell us about them?" Elisabeth asked.

"They're a Filipino gang primarily based in San Francisco. Over the past few years, they've been producing meth in labs in the remote areas outside of Sonoma."

"I should have guessed they'd be meth dealers like the Bagsics," Elisabeth said.

"A few months ago, the FBI stopped the Tumibays from receiving an incoming supply of ephedrine to the Port of San Francisco, so their meth trade has suffered. But two weeks ago, the Sacramento police intercepted a large shipment of Tumibay meth heading north. They don't know where the Tumibays got the ephedrine."

Elisabeth's eyes found Liam's, and she knew he was thinking the same thing. Did this have to do with the shipping container that Tomas had lost? But wouldn't the Bagsics have their shipments come into the Port of Los Angeles, not San Francisco?

"How did the Tumibays find you?" Detective Carter asked.

Liam's mouth hardened. "They had staked out Brady's house and followed us when we left."

The skin around the detective's eyes tightened. "That means…your father…"

"Could you have a squad car watch his house?" Liam asked.

"Not a problem. But I don't have jurisdiction to order an officer to watch out for Brady here in Geyserville, where the police force is stretched thin right now."

Liam nodded. "Elisabeth and I have already arranged to stay with him."

"Good." The detective relaxed.

But Elisabeth didn't. The guilt gnawed at her. She was used to protecting women and children, not making people targets. It had been one thing when the danger was only to herself and Liam, but now the gangs had pulled his family into the mix. They were being boxed in by wolves who were circling, getting ready to attack.

"Will you two be all right?" There was genuine concern in the detective's gray eyes. In working with him at the shelter, Elisabeth had always respected him professionally, but now he felt more like a friend. And she hadn't let herself have many friends for the past several years.

"We'll be careful," she said, and Liam nodded agreement.

After the detective had left, Liam took her aside. "The Tumibays are involved in why Joslyn is on the run from Tomas."

"And it might not be because of her father's murder, but because of that shipping container," she said, nodding in agreement. "We have to look into it."

"If we can't nail Tomas for the murder, maybe we can nail him on something to do with that shipping container."

Elisabeth glanced at the policemen wrapping up their work at the gas station. "I think they'll let us leave soon.

I'm worried about your brother and his wife. The Tumibays know where your family lives."

"Let's go back to Brady's house. We can't protect him at work, but we can at least be at the house with Debra and Ryan. We can call Shaun to give him the heads-up about Dad's house, and while we're at Brady's, we can do some research."

After Elisabeth remembered to fill up the gas tank, they drove back to Brady's house. Instead of parking in their driveway, Liam directed her to a nearby dirt access road about a hundred yards away from the back of the house.

"Their driveway only has one exit." Liam got his things out of the car and led the way across Brady's backyard, spacious with a large garden plot and a small pond. "And there's trees and bushes on either side of the driveway, so if the gang blocks the entrance to it, we'll need a different escape route."

As Elisabeth followed Liam, she realized another advantage to hiding their car. The gang wouldn't know right away that they were here. If they checked the garage, they'd only see Liam's brother's cars.

They crossed the lawn, passing a large fir tree strung with Christmas lights, surrounded by trimmed rosebushes rather haphazardly decorated with more lights. Elisabeth didn't know Brady or Debra well, but she guessed that while Debra had done the decorations in the living room and front door, Brady had done these.

Debra answered their knock at the back door. "Come on in. Where did you park?" There was that faint air of resentment despite her polite words. Elisabeth supposed she didn't like strangers in her home, or perhaps she simply didn't like disruptions to her scheduled plans.

"On the access road. It leaves your driveway clear," Liam answered.

"Whatever you like. Just don't track in mud from the garden."

Elisabeth followed Debra through the kitchen toward the guest bedrooms. The one-story home was built as a square with a spacious central courtyard including planted fruit trees. The guest bedrooms were next to each other and the hallway bathroom. The rooms had been decorated in shades of sand and taupe, matching Elisabeth's apartment decor. As she saw the room now, she realized how arid and lifeless the color scheme was. Perhaps she ought to redecorate her home when this was all over.

Would it ever be over? She was exhausted from the adrenaline rushes of the past few days coupled with little sleep. Yet Liam still looked strong and alert. And he hadn't lost that protectiveness over her. Strangely, she'd gotten used to it.

When this was over, her life could go back to normal. Safe. Predictable.

Isolated.

Was that what it really was? Was that what she really wanted?

Liam looked strangely hesitant as he stood in front of Debra, who had her arms folded in front of her. "Debra, did you have any plans to go out today?"

Her eyes narrowed. "I need to go grocery shopping."

"It may not be safe—"

"This again? You admitted you didn't know if the two men at your father's home were connected to the gang that's after you."

"Two gang members just attacked us at the gas station down the road. They told us they followed us from your house."

Debra started. "What do you mean? What kind of trouble have you brought on us, Liam? Why can you never keep any of your business to yourself?"

Liam's eyes fell and a muscle flexed in his jaw, indicating that her words held some deeper meaning for him. It was strange how Liam was so easy and friendly with Brady, and yet he and Debra circled each other like Siamese fighting fish.

Liam opened his mouth to speak, but Elisabeth forestalled him. "Debra, we're so sorry for all the inconvenience we're causing for you. Our jobs involve protecting people, and right now we just want to protect you and your baby."

Liam's grateful look warmed Elisabeth, although she looked away quickly. She focused on Debra's pinched expression rather than how Liam made her feel.

"You really are making things difficult for me." Debra's tone was petulant, but she was also a little less belligerent than before.

"We're sorry. If you could stay home only for the next day or two…" Realistically, they wouldn't be able to continue in this situation much longer than that.

Debra sighed. "Fine. I suppose I can go shopping tomorrow."

They'd deal with it then, Elisabeth supposed. "We don't want to get in your way. Is there somewhere we can get online?"

"You can use Brady's office."

Brady's office faced the backyard, with a soothing view of the lawn, trees and pond. The room was meticulously neat, but there were also stacks of folders on tables and bookcase shelves. "What does Brady do?" Elisabeth asked Liam.

"He's a forensic accountant. He investigates finances and fraud. He invited me to join his investigations firm when I came back from Afghanistan, but…" Liam grimaced. "I prefer less sedentary investigations, I guess."

She wasn't surprised to hear it. Elisabeth had noticed

that he was most comfortable when in motion, though he was clearly capable of focusing on intense computer work. She admitted that he was better at the computer research, whereas her strength in her investigations was interviews. In that sense, as they were looking into Joslyn and Tomas, they complemented each other.

She shook her head. She had to stop thinking like that.

"Let me call Shaun." Liam got out his cell phone and told him about the attack over speakerphone.

"Don't worry, I'll keep us safe." There was a steely confidence in Shaun's voice, and Elisabeth could imagine he had been a formidable border patrol officer. "Dad's got a good security system, and we'll be careful."

Liam visibly relaxed at his brother's words. "Thanks."

"Just…take care of yourself and Elisabeth, all right?" The concern in Shaun's voice made Elisabeth look away. Shaun was a stranger to her, and yet he'd thought of her. With the brutality of her life, and the way she'd protected herself, the kindness of others crept through a chink in her armor, catching her off guard.

After hanging up, Liam dialed Brady's number at his office. "Maybe I can convince him to work from home for the next few days. He doesn't have great security in the building where his office is."

"Are there are a lot of people around? The gang members might not do anything to him with so many witnesses."

"True. He's also in the middle of Geyserville. There are traffic and security cameras." Liam put his phone on speaker. "Hey, Brady."

While Liam explained again what had happened, Elisabeth glanced around the office. In addition to the file folders, Brady had lots of pictures of his brothers, his wife and son, and what looked to be some extended-family photos.

She liked the ones with all the O'Neill men, because they always seemed to be laughing together over something.

At Liam's father's house, the closeness between Liam, his brother and his father had unexpectedly touched her. She dealt with so many women with no one to turn to, and Elisabeth herself had no close family. Seeing Liam's family's love for each other, their teasing and playful interaction, had given her a glimpse into what she might be missing.

Even Liam's interactions with Brady, despite Debra's coolness, showed how much the two brothers cared for each other. She had known that kind of relationship existed, but she'd never seen it firsthand. And it made her feel strange.

Lonely.

She turned her attention back to Liam's conversation. Brady was surprised, but he took the threat more seriously than his wife had. "But I can't leave my office today, Liam. I'm meeting with a deputy attorney general about a case."

"Well, we're here with Debra and Ryan, so you won't need to worry about them."

"Thanks, bro." There was relief and warmth in Brady's voice.

"Brady, when you're ready to go home—"

"I'll try to come home early, and I'll ask a security guard to walk me to my car. I'll be careful."

When Liam hung up, she blurted, "You're really close with your family."

A glow came into his dark blue eyes. "I guess so. We drive each other crazy, but we're always there for each other." He regarded her for a moment, and it was as if he saw inside her. "Are you close to your family?"

She looked away. "No." Her voice came out snappish, and she regretted it. He had only asked an innocent question after all. She added in a softer tone, "I'm an only child. My mother died when I was sixteen, and…I was never close to my father. If I have any extended family, I don't know about them."

Liam's brow wrinkled. "You never looked?"

"I looked up my mother's family, but couldn't access the records in the Philippines." She hadn't bothered to try to find her father's family.

"I'm sorry." He looked stricken. "I'm always so annoyed by my family, I've never thought about…not having anyone."

She didn't want his pity. She needed to be strong, because she'd learned the hard way that it was the way to survive. "Don't be sorry," she said. Desperate to change the subject, she looked around. "Where should I set up?"

Liam ended up seated at Brady's desk while Elisabeth sat at a small circular table in the corner of the office. She opened her laptop. "So here's the question of the day: Why do the Tumibays want Joslyn?"

Liam leaned back in Brady's leather chair. "They might want her simply because they know the Bagsics want her. They could get leverage with the Bagsics if they have Joslyn, knowing Tomas would give up a lot to have her. But that Tumibay also knew about the shipping container that Tomas lost. What does that have to do with Joslyn and the murder?"

"And how did a San Francisco gang find out about a Bagsic shipping container in L.A.? Maybe these are two unrelated things, but they're both tied to Tomas."

"You think Tomas might be after Joslyn for something to do with the shipping container rather than because of the murder?"

She shrugged. "It's possible. They sent in a cleaner to the murder scene, and apparently they have a lawyer who has gotten gang members off from murder charges in the past. They don't seem to have much to worry about in terms of the murder, so why all this effort to find Joslyn?"

"I'll look for the ship and the shipping container," Liam said. "I think you said it was called the *Pansit?*"

"That's what the Bagsic at the club said. I'll look up that Tumibay gang member who attacked us, Lamar Garcia."

The first time they'd been working side by side like this, at her apartment, she'd been distracted by the fact that he was there in her personal space, at her dining room table. He had made her nervous.

Now their working together made her feel like part of a team. There were moments she felt that way when she worked with some staff at the shelter or when she was contracting with law enforcement. But this was different. She felt like a vital part of a whole. It made her feel needed in a way she hadn't felt before.

And it was because of Liam, because he respected her. Because he was almost someone she could trust.

"I've got nothing." Liam threw down the pen he'd been using to take notes and flung himself against the back of the chair. "There's no record of a ship called the *Pansit* ever docking in the Port of Los Angeles."

She was surprised. He'd been on the phone, making calls down to L.A., and she had assumed he'd find out something. "They might have found a way to keep it off the records."

Liam rubbed his hand across his face. "Some of the skip tracers I know wouldn't hesitate to break a few laws to find out. And I have to admit, the more frustrated I get, the more tempted I am to bend some rules."

She could hear the frustration in his voice, and at the same time, there was a noble quality to it. "But you won't do it."

"But I won't do it."

She respected that about him. She paused, then asked, "What keeps you from doing it?"

He didn't answer her right away. Finally he said, in a halting voice, "I know God wouldn't want me to. I don't want to disappoint Him."

She'd known he was a Christian, but she'd never heard him speak of God like this before. "Do you really think God cares about something so insignificant as finding a ship from the Philippines?"

"It's not insignificant to us. And yes, I do think He cares."

"Then I think that there are more important things that He should care about." Her voice came out sharper than she'd intended, but she couldn't help it. She thought about the loss and pain and betrayal in her life. Where had God been then? Why hadn't He considered it significant enough to save her?

"He cares about those, too." Liam's blue gaze was steady on her face, not self-righteous or judgmental, but kind. He was certainly different from other Christians she'd known.

She was embarrassed at how she'd lashed out at his faith. What had he ever done to her to deserve that kind of derision? "It's just that…you make it sound like you and God are best buds. It's strange to me." And why couldn't God have been best buds with her? Was there something wrong with her? Was it because she hadn't made good choices in her life? Was she being punished?

She sighed. What was she doing, inferring some deep theology from Liam's innocent words?

"He is my best bud," Liam said slowly. "It's what it's supposed to mean to be a Christian."

"Not to any of the other Christians I've known."

"Well, Christians aren't perfect. If they were, they wouldn't need God."

That hadn't really occurred to her. The conversation

was getting uncomfortable. She made it a policy not to talk about religion with people, mostly because she didn't want to think about religion herself. She cleared her throat. "Anyway, I think I found Joslyn's connection to the Tumibays."

Liam took the change in conversation in stride. "Oh?"

"I found several pictures of Lamar Garcia on social media. He posed in a few photos at a party with a guy named Daniel. But what's interesting is that in a different photo at the same party, Daniel is posing with a girl named Faye Torres. It looks like they're dating. Faye's name sounded familiar, so I looked at my notes on Joslyn. Faye is Joslyn's cousin."

"Joslyn was dating a Bagsic and her cousin is dating a Tumibay? What are the odds of that?"

"I think that Tomas pursued Joslyn—I don't think she actively wanted to date a gang member. Faye, on the other hand, looks like she's been wanting to be involved with the Tumibays for a while. From what I could find on her, she looks like she attended a lot of parties with other Tumibays and flirted around before meeting Daniel."

"Why would she want to do that?" Liam looked faintly disgusted.

Elisabeth shrugged. "Some women like the power associated with gang members. Their confidence makes them attractive."

"Do we know that Joslyn would go to her cousin for help? What if they weren't close?"

"They were close enough." Elisabeth clicked back to the photo of Joslyn at her workplace. "Do you see this user who commented, Fairydust9437? That's Faye. I saw her use it on another website. She wrote here, 'Nice photo, Joslyn! Is that Tomas? Wow, he's a cutie.'"

"So she knew Joslyn was dating a Bagsic. If Joslyn was betrayed by her boyfriend, I could see her jumping ship to another gang for protection, especially if her cousin had ties to it."

"But then why didn't Joslyn stay with Tumibays? Why are the Tumibays after her now?"

Liam's face grew dark. "Even if she said she wanted to align herself with them, the Tumibays might be ruthless enough that they'd turn around and sell her back to the Bagsics. She could have run from them to protect herself."

"And obviously Faye doesn't know where Joslyn is, or they wouldn't have needed to question me."

"We can't question Faye about Joslyn, either. There's too big a risk that she'd betray us to her boyfriend's gang."

At that moment, Debra appeared in the doorway, her face white. "You have to do something."

"What is it?" Liam rose to his feet. Elisabeth also stood.

Debra pointed toward the back of the house. "I was washing dishes at the sink, and I saw… I just saw two strange men sneak into the backyard."

TEN

At Debra's words, Liam's entire body shocked to life. "Debra, go through the house and shut off the lights." He grabbed his firearm from his laptop case.

Liam headed for the kitchen and snapped off the light. There was a window at the sink, but there was also a large window in a breakfast nook, opposite the table. He positioned himself beside the larger window and peeked out.

Dusk was falling—he hadn't realized it was so late. However, the Christmas lights he'd noticed earlier gave off a soft glow.

Elisabeth came up behind him so silently that he didn't realize she was there until she spoke. "Are there men out there?" She also had her gun, her body tense as she positioned herself on the other side of the window and looked out. "I don't see them."

"Where's Debra?"

"I told her to take Ryan into the study and hide under the desk."

They watched the backyard, and Liam's eyes gradually became accustomed to the dimness. They waited, and Liam was about to give up when he suddenly saw a shadow move between two fir trees.

"There are people out there," Elisabeth whispered. "I'll

call 9-1-1. I didn't want to do it earlier in case it was a false alarm."

She grabbed the phone in the kitchen and made the call. Liam only listened with half an ear as he scanned the backyard for any more movement. Switching off all the house lights must have alerted the intruders because they weren't making any moves toward the house.

Elisabeth came back to the window. "We only have to hold them off until the police arrive."

"Brady's house is on the edge of Geyserville, so if there aren't any cruisers nearby, it might take some time."

"Does the house have a security alarm? Maybe if we set it, the noise will scare them off."

Liam shook his head. His brother hadn't gotten around to getting an alarm system yet.

"How do you want to do this?" she asked.

"If I was going to approach the house, I could use the trees as cover until I reached the edge of the patio, then make a run for the side door. Or I could run across the lawn to the other side, then take cover in the bushes, which would hide me almost all the way to the sliding glass door at that corner of the house."

"So we wait to see what they do? How many are there?"

"As far as I can tell, only two. If they split up, I'll take the sliding glass door, you take the side door. It's in the laundry room." The laundry room had several spaces where a small figure could hide in wait. He wouldn't fit in those places, but she could.

She nodded. Then she holstered her gun. "We shouldn't use our firearms."

Because of the danger of stray bullets for Debra and Ryan. He grabbed one of Debra's kitchen knives and she took a cast-iron skillet.

They waited, watching the backyard. The minutes ticked by. Each one felt like an hour. Liam forced his heart rate to slow, become steady. Finally, they saw one man dart across the exposed area of the lawn while a shadow moved between the trees toward the side door. They were splitting up.

Liam hurried to the living room, avoiding the windows so the men outside wouldn't see him. Hopefully he could take care of the man there quickly so he could help Elisabeth with the other one.

Or maybe *she'd* take care of her attacker first and come to *Liam's* rescue. He wished he'd seen her when she'd fought Lamar Garcia at the gas station, but he'd heard her describe breaking his arm when the police officer took her statement.

He hid in the shadows of the living room, with a clear view of the sliding glass door, but unseen from outside. He didn't have long to wait before a man's figure appeared. He studied the glass door, then laid something on the ground—his gun. He grabbed the door handle and gave a powerful jerk. The first time didn't work, since the sliding glass door was relatively new and tight in the frame, but his second attempt lifted the door off the track so that he could drag it open.

He was still unarmed.

Liam rushed forward and tackled him, hurtling them both out onto the flagstone patio. They hit the stone with a jaw-clacking thud, and he lost his knife.

The man lashed out at Liam. He was quick and wiry. Liam blocked an elbow to his head and managed a solid blow to the man's torso that made his attacker pause.

Liam rose onto his knees and rained a hail of punches to the man's head. He blocked the first few, but then his defense started to sag as Liam's attacks connected with his head.

And then suddenly a heavy body crashed into him, sending Liam flying sideways. His head bounced hard off the flagstones, making stars explode in his vision.

There was a third man.

The weight across his torso and legs indicated a man who was heavier than Liam, but the attacker was also slower. Liam kicked out with a leg and connected with the man's thigh, then rolled away, trying to still his spinning head. The third man grabbed at his legs, holding him on the ground. Liam struggled and tried to kick again, but the man's meaty hands held him fast.

So he crunched up into a sitting position and swung at the man's unprotected head. He couldn't see well in the dimness, but his fists landed on a fleshy cheek, an ear, his nose, and smashed into the man's mouth. The man let go of Liam and rolled away.

Liam sprang to his feet, but froze when a voice said, "Hold it right there."

The smaller man held his gun pointed at Liam. He recognized him now as Lamar Garcia, the man from the gas station, in the leather jacket and with the fishhook scar on his face. However, Liam didn't recognize the larger man, who got clumsily to his feet. He was a mountain of a man, with wide shoulders, beefy arms and a barrel torso.

"You said it was only the woman and the baby home," the larger man said to his partner, his voice deep and sulky with accusation.

"I checked the garage," Garcia snapped. "They must have parked somewhere else."

But the advantage of surprise hadn't done Liam much good. How long before the police arrived? Liam had thought they'd want to capture him and ask him questions, but the man held the gun at him, face tense. He looked as if he was going to shoot. Would he risk the neighbors hearing the gunshot?

Liam stared down the barrel of the gun. The man was close; he wouldn't miss. And then Liam felt a wave of peace wash over him. The situation was in God's hands, not his.

He exhaled slowly, and somehow knew he would be okay.

"Freeze!" It was Elisabeth's voice.

Liam turned and saw her coming from around the side of the house. Her hair was wild around her head, but her hands were steady as she aimed her firearm at the two men. "Drop the gun." She must have taken out the other attacker.

"Drop yours or I'll shoot him," Garcia said, his hand steady as he held his gun.

There was a wavering in her determined face.

"Don't think about me," Liam told her. "Just don't let them get away."

And then he heard it—the faint wail of a police siren.

"Drop the gun," Elisabeth repeated.

This time, it was Garcia who wavered.

"Come on!" a man's voice shouted behind Elisabeth, and she spun around. The man she had taken out at the side door must have come to, because he staggered around the corner, but he yelped and jumped back when he saw Elisabeth pointing her gun at him.

"Let's go," the big man said to Garcia.

"The police aren't here yet. She's right there—"

"We have to go or the car'll be trapped in the driveway." The large man turned and ran around the side of the house, heading toward the front. Elisabeth's attacker followed him.

Garcia shot Liam an angry, frustrated look, then he also turned and ran.

Liam raced after him.

Garcia turned and fired back a wild gunshot. Liam ducked and swerved, taking cover behind the corner of the house. He peeked around before pursuing the men.

He saw headlights swing across the front of the house, illuminating the trees that lined the driveway. The police already? But there were no flashing lights and he could still hear the sirens at a distance.

And then he realized. *Brady.*

He hadn't told Brady not to come home.

"Brady!" His shout scraped against his throat.

"Hey!" It was his brother's voice.

Liam turned the corner of the house in time to see Brady throw himself at Garcia as he ran past. The two flew farther down the driveway, rolling on the ground, and Liam saw the man's gun go flying.

Brady had been a wrestler in high school, and recently he'd been going to the mixed martial arts gym with Liam. He grappled with the man with powerful arms and landed a few punches to the man's side.

Liam had almost reached them when Garcia slashed out and Brady jerked backward with a cry. The faint light glinted gray off the blade of a knife.

"Brady!" Liam ran to where his brother lay curled on the ground. He spared only a glance for Garcia as he fled into the gang's getaway car.

The sirens were coming closer, but they wouldn't arrive before the men had exited Brady's long driveway.

Liam knelt in front of his brother. Seconds later, Elisabeth appeared at his side.

"Brady, are you all right?"

Brady grimaced and rolled toward him. The pale sleeve of his button-down shirt was soaked with a wet, warm patch, dark and running from his shoulder to his elbow.

Blood.

Liam applied pressure to the knife wound on his brother's shoulder with shaking hands. It had been one thing to have a gun pointed directly at him; it was another thing entirely to watch Brady bleed all over his driveway.

The strange peace he'd felt only moments ago, when the man had aimed the gun at him, had completely deserted him now. He would do everything he could to stop these men, to prevent something like this from happening again.

The police came up the driveway, sirens screaming. As an officer walked toward them, the front door opened and Debra ran out of the house with Ryan in her arms. "Help us! Help!" The officer went to intercept her.

"Call the paramedic!" Liam shouted.

A second officer nodded and spoke into his radio.

His brother's eyes were open but bright with pain, stress lines visible along the side of his mouth.

Liam forced himself to speak with a teasing tone. "You're such a wimp."

Brady grimaced, but then he smiled. "I've had worse. Remember the time Shaun dared me to climb on that tractor and I fell and gashed open my leg?"

Liam winced. "I can't believe we were ever that stupid."

When the paramedics arrived, they worked on Brady while Liam and Elisabeth gave their statements to the officers.

"Were these the same men from the gas station earlier today?" The officer taking Liam's statement had also responded to the gas station attendant's 9-1-1 call.

"Yes, one of the men was Lamar Garcia. I don't know about the other two—I didn't get a good look at them."

They'd been lucky. It had been just himself and Elisabeth against three men. They'd also been able to surprise them since the men had obviously thought they'd only had Debra and Ryan to deal with. God had been watching out for his family tonight.

Debra had taken one look at Brady's arm and blanched, so she spent most of her time, after giving her statement to the police officer, pacing in front of the house with Ryan in her arms. Except for one moment, right after the officer had finished taking Liam's statement.

She marched up to Liam. "You did this." Her voice was

full of venom, and her eyes were wild. Her hysterical mood had affected Ryan, who was crying. "You brought those men to our home. You're the reason Brady is injured. I hope you're happy." Then she stalked away.

Liam had stood there a moment, surprised at her attack, which cut deeply because he knew she was right. He should have prevented this. He shouldn't have assumed there were only two men. He should have worked harder to fight the big man off and secure the gun.

Elisabeth came up to him then. "Stop it."

"What?"

"Stop blaming yourself. You couldn't have predicted what would happen."

He could have. He was sure of it. She was trying to make him feel better, but he knew this was his fault. And only he could fix things.

The paramedics took Brady to the hospital, and Liam drove Debra, Elisabeth and Ryan there in Debra's car. While Debra was with Brady and the doctor, Shaun arrived.

"How's he doing?" Shaun was serious but calm, in contrast with how agitated Liam felt.

"Paramedics said they think he'll be fine. The wound wasn't deep." Liam frowned. "Did you bring Dad?"

"No, I left him at home, but I asked Nathan to stay and watch over him and Monica. And Detective Carter sent a police officer to watch the house, too."

Liam sighed in relief. After Brady's attack, the last thing he wanted was to worry about one of the gangs going after his father. He realized that he felt guilty not only for the attack at Brady's house, but also for the fact that these events would only worry Shaun and his father, both of them already stressed by Dad's chemo treatments. Hadn't his whole intention been to not burden his family, not with his own mental problems, and certainly not with an investigation?

"Do you think they'll attack Brady or Dad's house again?" Shaun asked.

"Who knows? Although they got onto Brady's property pretty easily."

Shaun frowned. "I keep telling him to get that security system in place. He's always saying he'll do it soon, but he's been busy with work lately. And…" Shaun cut himself off, his eyes flickering to Liam.

"Yeah, I asked him about Debra, but he didn't want to talk about it."

Shaun blew out a frustrated breath. "I wish he'd just talk to us. We're his family. We might be able to help."

Liam snorted. "O'Neill men are not great talkers. You know that."

Shaun smiled ruefully. "Well, he shouldn't have to deal with this alone."

"It didn't help that I asked him to move in with Dad for a few days. Debra almost bit my head off."

Shaun's eyes narrowed. "She might think differently now. Want me to talk to her?"

"Could you? I'm not her favorite person." The echo of her words still had the power to cut him, like little razors over his skin.

Shaun nodded and headed to Brady's bedside. Liam went back to the waiting area.

Elisabeth sat with her laptop. "I hope it doesn't seem callous of me to be working, but I figured since we were waiting…"

"It's great. The sooner we can figure this out, the better." It was the only way he could think of to keep his family safe. "Found anything?"

"I'm doing more research into Faye, Joslyn's cousin, and her Tumibay connections. I think I found one of the men who attacked us." She showed him a candid photo of the man at a club in San Francisco.

"That looks like the big guy who attacked me. What's his name?"

"The website only gives a nickname, Sneezy."

Liam groaned. "Seven Dwarves, really?"

"My FBI contacts have told me that every gang has members nicknamed after the Seven Dwarves."

It was nice to joke with her like this, to alleviate the strain of the past couple hours. To forget about Brady's blood, Debra's barbs.

At that moment, her cell phone rang. She blinked at the caller ID. "It's Mariella. Hello?" She listened for a few moments, then suddenly straightened in her chair. "What?... How did you—?...Are you sure?"

"What is it?" Liam asked. He wished she'd put the call on speakerphone.

Elisabeth then gave a rueful smile. It brought a rose color to her cheeks. Liam wanted to touch her face.

"All right," she said to Mariella. "I'll tell him. 'Bye. And thanks."

"Next time—"

"I know," she interrupted him. "Next time I'll put it on speakerphone. You guessed right. Mariella didn't listen to you. She went looking into the information we found out at the club."

Liam groaned. "I wish you hadn't told her what those gang members said to each other in Filipino."

"Well, in this case, it paid off. She found the *Pansit*."

Liam gaped. "How?"

"It's like we were suspecting, someone kept it off the shipping records. But Mariella has a second cousin's roommate who's related to someone who works at the port authority—something convoluted like that—and she found out that the *Pansit* originated from the Philippines. There's no documentation on it in the U.S., but she verified its arrival through the documentation in the Philippines.

And, Liam, the *Pansit* docked two days after Joslyn's father was killed."

That couldn't be a coincidence. "So that shipping container that Tomas lost—was that related to the murder? Was Joslyn's father involved somehow, and killing him caused Tomas to lose it? We've been thinking, from what Joslyn told you and the women at the shelter, that she was running from Tomas because of her father's murder. But what if it was something else, something to do with that shipping container?"

"We've also been assuming Tomas needs Joslyn for some reason. What if she did something against the gang, and Tomas wants her back for revenge?"

Liam had a sinking feeling in his gut. "If that's the case, then finding out the truth about the murder isn't going to give us anything we can use against Tomas—or anything to stop the Tumibays."

Elisabeth's chin firmed. "We have to find a way to stop both gangs, or we'll be running from them forever, and the threat to your family won't go away."

"Maybe we can still find some proof to pin the murder on Tomas—no matter what his reasons, he still did kill a man. And then we can find something else to get the Tumibays off our backs."

"To stop them, we need to know why the Tumibays want Joslyn. We have to follow her trail from when her father was killed until she came to the shelter. From what those gang members said, Joslyn had to have interacted with the Tumibays at some point."

At that moment, Shaun appeared, carrying his nephew, asleep on his shoulder. He gestured with his head to Liam.

"I'll be right back," Liam told Elisabeth, and approached his brother.

"Brady's going to be fine." Shaun kept his voice pitched low so he wouldn't wake up Ryan. "He had a nasty cut, but they've sewn him up and pumped him full of antibiotics. They're going to discharge him soon."

"Good." Liam sighed. It had been so much blood...

"I also convinced Debra to stay with me and Dad."

"How did you do that?"

Shaun grinned. "My infamous charm."

"It's probably because you're not me," Liam said drily.

"Actually, she was pretty eager to move to Dad's after what happened."

"I wish she'd agreed earlier. Then Brady wouldn't have gotten hurt."

"Hey." Shaun clasped Liam's shoulder. "None of us could have known they'd do that. It's useless playing 'what if.' What we need to do now is take precautions to protect ourselves."

Liam pressed his lips together and nodded. He'd do everything he could to stop these men. He had to protect his family.

Shaun went back to Brady and Debra, and Liam told Elisabeth about Brady's family staying with his dad.

"That's great," she said enthusiastically. "Because I've found a new lead."

His heartbeat quickened. "What?"

"Do you remember when Nathan told you about that policeman reporting that he'd seen Joslyn at that bus stop a day after the murder?"

"Yeah, in central California somewhere."

"Paso Robles. She didn't get back on the bus. Guess where Faye's mother lives? After she was forced to leave the bus, I'm guessing she went to her aunt to help her travel north." Elisabeth gave him a smile. "Want to go on another road trip?"

ELEVEN

The next morning, as they drove south toward central California, the greater distance from Sonoma seemed to enable Elisabeth to distance herself from the conflicting feelings she'd been having.

She had told Liam not to blame himself, and yet the guilt weighed on her, too. Her involvement with Joslyn had brought all this trouble on Liam and his family. She shouldn't have agreed to work with him. If she'd left him alone, he'd have dropped Patricia's case once he knew she wasn't Joslyn's sister, and the gang would have left him alone.

Wouldn't they?

At the very least, the Tumibays wouldn't have attacked his family's homes. And she really liked his family. They shared a closeness she'd never seen with other people she'd known. They were committed to each other. They loved each other.

That kind of love was so foreign to her. While she'd been with the O'Neills, she'd started deceiving herself into thinking she could have a love like that, too, a family who would care about her. She'd been forgetting the hard lessons she'd had to learn at the hands of her father, and then her ex-boyfriend.

As she drove from Sonoma, the reality of her past, her

life, came back into focus. Who was she kidding? She couldn't have that. She wasn't made for that. It was better to remain alone and safe.

She glanced sideways at Liam, taking his turn driving her car. He was a better man than most of the people she'd known, but she still shouldn't rely on him too much. Depending on people had only gotten her hurt, and she wasn't about to subject herself to that kind of pain all over again.

Blanca Torres's home was a remodeled barn on the edge of a large vineyard. Chickens scattered in front of the car as they drove up to the house. Although they were not turned on, Elisabeth could see Christmas lights lavishly strung from the eaves, around windows, even around the front door. An artificial tree sat in front of the house, heavy with lights and multicolored ornaments.

They parked alongside a large pen where a dozen goats stared at them as they got out of the car. The smell was ripe and musty and grassy at the same time, and Elisabeth coughed.

"This is a long drive for one conversation," Liam muttered as they looked around the deserted yard.

"I do better with face-to-face talks, especially if the person isn't likely to want to help me." Elisabeth caught sight of movement on the other side of the goat pen. "And something tells me Joslyn's aunt isn't going to want to admit she had any interaction with a niece wanted by the police for questioning."

They headed toward the side of the house, circling the goat pen. The smell of goat was strong, but as they kept walking she began to be aware of a pungent, fishy smell that hung heavy in the air. It reminded Elisabeth of British fish-and-chips from a diner she'd gone to once, and it also brought up an older memory, something that teased the back of her mind. It made her think of the old calamansi lemon tree that had grown in her mother's backyard, the big plastic doghouse she'd commandeered as her playhouse, the clotheslines strung from the aluminum patio roof to the fence where her father's white undershirts swayed under a hot California sun.

They turned a corner and saw a weathered Filipino woman in a faded cotton apron sitting on a low wooden stool. In front of her was a propane burner with a large metal wok, filled with oil. She was frying fish.

Elisabeth didn't want to startle her, not with the wok of boiling oil in front of her. "Mrs. Torres?" she asked quietly.

But the woman must have seen their car come up the driveway, because she didn't even turn to look at them. "What do you want?" Using long metal tongs, she flipped a piece of fish.

Elisabeth switched to Tagalog. "My name is Elisabeth Aday, and I'm a friend of your niece, Joslyn."

The brown hand holding the metal tongs paused, then she continued flipping the fish in the wok. "What do you want with me?" Her voice was more wary, but she responded in Tagalog.

"I can assure you, we're not the police."

At this, Mrs. Torres glanced at them, her beady black eyes studying Liam for a long moment before she turned back to her fish.

Elisabeth continued, "I know you have no reason to believe me, but Joslyn came to a shelter I work at in Sonoma, and I helped her escape her ex-boyfriend."

Mrs. Torres swiveled fully around on her stool. "Let me see your card."

Elisabeth fished out a business card from her purse and gave it to her. Liam followed suit. The woman studied the cards with a frown creasing her tanned face.

"What's the name of the shelter?" Mrs. Torres suddenly asked.

"Wings shelter. It's not very well-known because it's for women escaping especially dangerous abusers."

At the name, Mrs. Torres's strong fingers twitched. If Joslyn went to her aunt for help, there was a good chance she'd mentioned the name of the shelter she was trying to reach.

"I've heard of it," Mrs. Torres said. Was there a softer tone to her voice? Then she remembered her fish, and with a little yelp, she grabbed her tongs and checked them. She began stacking the pieces on top of each other in the wok.

To drain the excess oil. Elisabeth suddenly remembered her mother doing the same thing, except she had used an electric burner sitting on a cinder block rather than a propane burner. There had been a heavy-duty electrical cord running from the inside of the house, through the crack in the sliding screen door. The images came to her in a flash, along with the remembered smell of frying oil and fish.

"My mom used an electric burner to fry her fish," she said to Mrs. Torres.

The woman's eyebrows rose. "Propane is hotter. Did she use a wok?"

"No, a cast-iron pot."

Mrs. Torres nodded thoughtfully. "That works, too. What kind of fish?"

"Whatever she could get. She liked pompano the best."

"Pompano is always the best." Mrs. Torres looked approving. She laid her fried fish in a metal baking sheet lined with paper towels, then turned off her burner. Gathering up her fish and tongs, she rose. "Come inside for coffee."

Elisabeth let out a low, relieved breath, then followed Mrs. Torres into a side door into the farmhouse.

The interior looked like a classic farmhouse, except that religious pictures of crosses and Jesus dotted the walls and sat on bookshelves. Bright red and green Christmas decorations were hung around the room—wreaths on the walls, garlands over doorways and a Christmas tree in the living room with a worse-for-wear angel at the top that was tilted sideways because it was a little too tall for the ceiling.

Mrs. Torres had them sit at a worn wooden table in the kitchen while she set the fish on the counter to cool. She started the coffeemaker and set out some homemade *paciencia,* Filipino meringue cookies, on a plate in front of Liam and Elisabeth.

Elisabeth hadn't had *paciencia* in years. The sweet meringue crumbled and melted on her tongue.

"You're a good cook," she said to Mrs. Torres.

Mrs. Torres waved a dismissive hand to her, but Elisabeth caught the pleased smile on her face.

"My mom used to make *paciencia* the week before Christmas."

Mrs. Torres nodded. "I always make for Christmas."

Elisabeth sat and listened to Mrs. Torres talk about the family parties, which inevitably involved lots of Filipino food. Elisabeth glanced at Liam, who must be bored since he couldn't understand Tagalog, but he was enjoying his coffee and cookies.

"My daughter drives me down to Los Angeles," Mrs. Torres said. "All our family is there."

"Faye lives in San Francisco?"

"Yes, she has a good job working in an insurance company. But she's lonely. She needs a boyfriend."

Elisabeth continued smiling, though she wanted to frown. So Faye's mother didn't know about her Tumibay boyfriend. Maybe not even her Tumibay connections. Had she known about Joslyn's Bagsic ex-boyfriend?

"Is Faye close to Joslyn?"

Mrs. Torres hesitated, then said, "Yes, because they're the closest in age out of all the cousins."

Elisabeth touched Mrs. Torres's hand. "I'm sure Joslyn

was grateful to you and Faye for helping her run from her ex-boyfriend."

Mrs. Torres looked torn, as if unsure what to tell Elisabeth. "Faye will always help her cousin. She's just like that. She calls me every Sunday," she said in a brighter tone, changing the subject. "She tells me about her day."

"You talked to her this past Sunday? How is she?"

Mrs. Torres's eyes faltered and fell. "She…she didn't call."

"Maybe she was too busy?"

"She usually calls, although some weeks she doesn't if she's too busy. But…"

Elisabeth said gently, "Would you like me to check on her for you?"

Mrs. Torres gave a hesitant nod. "Yes, thank you." She sat in silence for a long moment, her face lined with worry. Then she whispered, "She was scared. Joslyn. She was afraid of her ex-boyfriend."

Elisabeth squeezed the woman's hand comfortingly.

"I lent her my car so she could drive to Faye's apartment. And then the police came, telling me about Felix's murder. And now Faye… She always calls me. Always." Mrs. Torres's hand trembled beneath Elisabeth's fingers.

"I'll do my best to find her and help her," Elisabeth said.

She had Mrs. Torres write down Faye's address, and she asked the woman to call Faye's roommate to let her know Elisabeth and Liam would be coming to look around Faye's room.

As they left, Mrs. Torres gave Elisabeth a small plastic container with more *paciencia* cookies.

"I'll call you when I find Faye."

Mrs. Torres still looked worried, but she clasped Elisabeth's hand in a strong grip. "Thank you."

As they drove away, Liam said, "That was a long conversation. What happened?"

Elisabeth took a deep breath. "I think something has happened to Faye."

* * *

Had the Tumibays or Bagsics done something to Faye? Was she even still alive?

Elisabeth recounted the conversation for Liam, remembering Mrs. Torres's anxiety for Faye. Mother and daughter were obviously close to each other.

"But Mrs. Torres didn't know Faye was dating a Tumibay?" Liam asked. "I suppose her mother wouldn't exactly approve of a gang member boyfriend. So Mrs. Torres sent Joslyn to Faye in San Francisco not knowing that Faye has connections to the Tumibays, which might put Joslyn in more danger. Did Joslyn go to the Tumibays willingly? Or not? Did Faye turn her in to the Tumibays or try to protect her from them?"

"But why would the Tumibays get involved with a woman wanted by the police?" Elisabeth asked. "And how did she get away? The Tumibays don't know where Joslyn is, which means Faye either doesn't know, or she didn't tell them. What if Faye *does* know where Joslyn is, and that's why she disappeared?"

Liam gave her a side glance and said quietly, "We don't know yet if she ran away, or if something happened to her."

Elisabeth didn't want to think about that grim possibility. "But I'm starting to think she did run away. She also disappeared only recently, but Joslyn's been gone for weeks. So maybe the gang found out she knew."

"One thing we do know, Faye might be the one person, besides Joslyn, who knows what's going on," Liam said. "But if she ran away, it might take a while to find her. Joslyn disappeared without a trace."

"But I trained Joslyn," Elisabeth said. "I didn't train Faye. And that's going to make a big difference."

They stopped at a fast-food restaurant with free Wi-Fi. Elisabeth went online and found out more about Faye's workplace.

"She trained as a PA," Elisabeth said, "and she's well paid at her job. She wouldn't just throw it away. Let's check there first."

They got to San Francisco in a couple hours and headed into downtown, parking a few blocks away from the office building.

They were walking toward the building and Liam was looking casually around when he suddenly stiffened. Then he smoothly guided them into a deli, keeping their backs to the large storefront windows.

Elisabeth ducked her head. "What is it?"

"Tumibay, I think. He's Filipino and he's got the same style tattoos."

"Where?"

"I saw him sitting at the bus stop directly across from the building. Where are you going?"

Elisabeth stepped out of the deli, keeping her back to the bus stop several yards away, and fished a compact out of her purse. She flipped it open and used the mirror to look over her shoulder.

The man lounged on the bus stop bench. He wore a San Francisco Giants sweatshirt, but had pushed up the cuffs to reveal tattoos on his forearms. Elisabeth recognized certain Baybayin letters as the same as the tattoos she'd seen on the other two Tumibay men at the gas station.

She went back inside the deli, where Liam was fuming. "Yup, Tumibay," she said.

He glared at her. "You're killing me here."

She really hadn't thought first about how her actions would make him worry. She wasn't used to someone else caring about her. It was a strange feeling. "Sorry," she murmured.

His eyes softened. "Next time, just tell me before you do it, okay?"

"Okay." Elisabeth chewed her lip. "If Faye did run away,

if she wasn't taken by the gang, then my guess is they're waiting for her to show up."

Liam craned his neck to look out the deli windows. "I think we can backtrack to the crosswalk, cross the street and walk into the building by hiding in a crowd."

They made an effort to stick close to masses of people, hiding in the midst of them. Liam was a bit tall, but with his baseball cap in place, he looked like any other tourist.

They were directly across the street from the Tumibay now. She didn't turn to look, her heartbeat as fast as if she'd run a seven-minute mile.

Finally they entered the office building's large, empty lobby. "Now I know why the gang member is across the street," she said. "There's no place to sit here. Just the bus stop."

"Lucky for us."

They were on the watch for gang members hanging around, but didn't see any. Even up on the seventh floor, the elevator bay had no one around. They went straight to the glass double doors for Dutton Investments, which took up most of the office space on this floor.

The entrance to the offices was a square room with couches and tables, and at the far end, across from the glass doors, was a wide reception desk. Elisabeth smiled at the pretty young woman who sat behind the desk. "How can I help you?"

"We're looking for Faye Torres? We're friends with her cousin."

"Oh, she's on indefinite leave. Her mother's really sick or was in an accident or something like that." The receptionist grimaced. "Poor thing."

"Oh, no, that's awful," Elisabeth said. "Did this just happen?"

"Last week. Faye came in to pick up her paycheck on

Friday and talk to our boss about it. She looked so worried, she was as white as a sheet. He let her go home right away."

"I'll be sure to give her family a call," Elisabeth said. "Thanks."

They were alone in the elevator on the way down. "She went on the run," Elisabeth said. "If she'd been taken by a gang, she wouldn't have been able to give notice."

"And the Tumibays are staking out her workplace, so they obviously haven't found her since she went into hiding," Liam said. "That's good news."

"It also answers the question of who she's running from. But why would she run from her boyfriend's gang?"

"She must have done something to upset them."

"But she seemed to want to join the Tumibays so much," Elisabeth said. "Why would she turn against them?"

Liam looked at her. "Family."

Of course, the most obvious answer. Elisabeth realized that since she didn't understand family loyalty, it was hard for her to get into Faye's head.

Liam said, "Didn't you say that Joslyn was close to Faye? What if Faye helped Joslyn escape from the Tumibays or something like that? It would explain why the Tumibays are after both of them."

Once in the lobby, they waited until they could mix in with a large group of people leaving the building. They made it to their parked car without incident.

"We'll have to be careful when we go to Faye's apartment," Elisabeth said.

"I think they won't have more than one man watching the apartment, if that." Liam started the engine. "Faye's been gone almost a week. I don't think they really expect her to show up at her work or home."

"How long would they keep this surveillance up for one woman?"

"It depends what she did to make them want to find her.

If it's important enough, they'll expend resources to find her like Tomas did for Joslyn."

And what would they do if they found her? Elisabeth suppressed a shiver.

Faye lived in south San Francisco in a building with shops on the first floor and apartments above. The only point of access to the apartments was the underground parking garage.

They parked in the garage, and Liam had just gotten out of the car when he froze. "Get down," he hissed.

Elisabeth had been about to stand up, but she huddled back down into the car seat. "Tumibay?"

Liam had folded into a crouch, and he looked toward the elevators through the windows of the car parked next to them. "He's in a black SUV with a clear view of the elevators."

Elisabeth raised her head to look and saw the truck. Unlike the other SUV at the gas station, this one had no detail work and blended in with the other cars. She didn't recognize the driver, but his arm hanging out the open window exposed his tattoos up his arm to the sleeve of his T-shirt. They were definitely Tumibay tattoos.

Incredibly, he was asleep, with his eyes closed, his head leaning back against the headrest and his mouth hanging open. In the quiet of the garage, they could hear his snores.

"Let's make a run for it," Liam said.

They got out of the car, quietly easing the car doors closed. Liam gave her a quick look, then hurried across the garage toward the elevators. The stairwell was right next to the elevators, so he opened the door and they slipped inside. Elisabeth heaved a quick breath as the door closed behind them.

When they knocked on the door to Faye's apartment, it was immediately opened by her roommate, a petite girl with incredibly curly black hair and large eyes.

"Gina?" Elisabeth asked. "I'm Elisabeth Aday, and this is Liam O'Neill."

"Mrs. Torres said you'd be stopping by. Come on in."

"Thanks." They stepped into the small living room, dominated by a floral couch across from a large-screen television.

"I hope you can find Faye." Gina led them through the apartment. "I'm really worried about her. I feel so guilty—I've been on the night shift at work for two weeks, so I didn't even know she was missing until Mrs. Torres called today."

"Did you know anything about her social life?" Elisabeth asked carefully. "Something she might not have told her mom?"

"Well…" Gina's dark eyes slipped away. "She was dating this one guy, Daniel, but to be honest, he kind of scared me. He was one of those tough guys with tattoos all over his arms."

"Do you know anything else about him?"

"Not really. He and Faye have been going out for only a few weeks, and he came to our apartment only once or twice." Gina frowned. "As far as I know, he hasn't come by looking for her. He might know what happened to Faye. Or else he's such a scumbag that he doesn't care she's been missing."

"Do you know his last name?" Liam asked.

"No, sorry." Gina opened Faye's bedroom door. "Just let yourselves out when you're done, the door will lock behind you. It's my bedtime—my shift starts at eight."

Elisabeth winced. "I hope you didn't stay up just for us."

"No, I always have a hard time sleeping during the day when I'm on night shift. It's only for another week."

Gina disappeared into the other bedroom, and Liam and Elisabeth looked around Faye's room.

There were a couple religious pictures on the wall that

were identical to those in her mom's house, but Faye also had a concert poster and some framed photos of herself with friends. A wall calendar was filled with Faye's appointments. Her bed was a rumpled mess, and her dresser drawers were all half-open, their contents spilling over the edges.

"It looks like she packed in a hurry," Elisabeth said.

Liam looked through her trash while Elisabeth went through Faye's small desk, but the drawers were filled with innocuous things like nail polish, nail files, nail polish remover, cotton balls and makeup. There was a filled check register but no checkbook, and a few bills stuffed into a bottom drawer.

Her closet was jammed to the brim with evening dresses, conservative office-appropriate clothes and some casual sportswear. Liam sifted through her nightstand while Elisabeth pulled some Christmas cards that Faye had stuck in the frames of her photos.

The cards were all simply signed with people's names except for one. It had a printed sheet inside that gave a summary of the family's year, and it was signed, "Love you, Faye! Solidad."

The name was familiar. Elisabeth went back to Faye's wall calendar, and saw that she had "Solidad, 1:00 p.m." scattered regularly throughout the calendar. When she flipped through the entire year, she saw that Faye had that appointment every third Thursday.

She scanned Solidad's family letter and saw that Solidad was a manicurist.

And today was Thursday.

"I know how to find Faye." Elisabeth showed Liam the appointment in the wall calendar. "She gets her nails done like clockwork every three weeks, and she's close enough friends with Solidad that the woman sent Faye a family letter. I think she'll be there today for her normal appointment."

Liam looked at her blankly. "Even though she's hiding from the Tumibays?"

"It's one place I guarantee you that Faye's boyfriend never went. Women can get very close to their hair stylists and their manicurists."

Liam nodded in understanding. "And Faye doesn't realize that any skip tracer would look for her through her interests. She wouldn't know to abandon all of them in order to stay off the grid."

"Let's go."

They exited the apartment, making sure the door was locked behind them, and headed downstairs. Once they reached the door to the parking garage, Liam hesitated with his hand on the doorknob. "Let's walk out casually. The Tumibay might still be asleep, or he might not yet know that his gang is after us."

Elisabeth nodded. Liam opened the door.

The Tumibay was not asleep. In fact, he was several yards directly ahead of them, with a cup of coffee in his hand, obviously freshly returned from a coffee shop. He glanced casually at them first, but then did a double take, his brows drawing low over his dark eyes. Then a slow smile spread across his mouth. "I know someone looking for you," he drawled.

Liam tossed the car keys at Elisabeth. "Run!"

Then he launched himself at the gang member.

TWELVE

Elisabeth sprinted for the car, jamming the keys into the lock and diving inside. She unlocked the passenger door but didn't open it. She started the engine and, with a desperate look behind her, shot backward out of the parking stall.

Tires squealed as she cranked the wheel left. The taillights illuminated Liam's form grappling with the gang member.

She didn't want to fire her gun because she wasn't sure she would hit the man and not Liam. Instead, she had a crazy idea.

She revved the engine and then gunned it, backing the car straight into the struggling men.

They both turned, their eyes wide in the light from her taillights. The gang member jerked backward, releasing Liam.

She slammed on the brakes inches before hitting them. The Tumibay scrambled away while Liam darted toward her, sliding over the back corner of the trunk to land on the passenger side. He pulled open the door and was barely inside before she put the car in Drive and zoomed out of the garage.

Elisabeth didn't realize how tightly she was gripping

the steering wheel until, several blocks away, Liam put his hand over hers. "We're okay."

She realized how fast she was going and slowed down. His thumb rubbed over her knuckles once, twice. The sensation calmed her. When he removed his hand, she immediately wanted him to touch her again.

"Nice driving back there, in the garage," he said.

"It was the only thing I could think of to make him let you go." She gave him a guilty look. "I know that was kind of crazy."

"It worked. I can't complain."

Liam looked up the address for Solidad's nail salon. It was in a small market square, each store alike with dark brown shingles on the roof and slightly dingy stucco walls. Solidad's Hair and Nails flashed in neon pink above the store.

They were careful to check for any Tumibay members who might have been watching the salon, but they saw no one.

"It probably wouldn't occur to Daniel that she'd keep her appointment even when she's in hiding," Liam said. "I'm still not entirely convinced she's here."

"I've known women like Faye." Elisabeth opened the glass door to the shop, peered inside, then gave Liam a triumphant smile.

The shop was very narrow, and Faye sat at a station near the back. Her shoulders drooped, and she looked worn and tired. Solidad was massaging Faye's hands and nodding as Faye seemed to be unburdening herself.

Liam gave Elisabeth a rueful look. "I stand corrected."

"I'm just glad she's still all right." Elisabeth entered the shop and went straight to Faye.

Joslyn's cousin stopped midsentence to gape up at Elisabeth. But rather than curiosity or surprise, there was fear in her brown eyes.

"It's all right," Elisabeth said quickly. "Your mother sent me to help you."

Faye's lower lip trembled, and then she burst into tears.

"Now see what you've done?" Solidad glared at Elisabeth and Liam even as she grabbed handfuls of tissues from a box on the table next to her and thrust them at Faye. "Sweetheart, you need to stop crying. You don't want your nose to turn red."

Faye's sobs calmed into hiccups within a few minutes. "Who are you? What do you want?" she asked.

"I'm Elisabeth Aday, a private investigator, and this is Liam O'Neill, a skip tracer. I helped your cousin Joslyn when she came to a women's shelter where I volunteer in Sonoma."

"Is she all right?" Faye's earnest tone and wide eyes made it obvious how much her cousin meant to her.

Elisabeth didn't want to lie to her, but she didn't want to worry her more. "I think so, but I also need your help to make sure she stays that way."

Faye's eyes darted around the tiny shop, and she licked her lips. "They're after me," she whispered.

"We can protect you," Liam said, and the solid confidence in his tone seemed to instill some courage in Faye.

Faye turned to Solidad. "Can we use your office?"

"Yes, yes." Solidad gestured impatiently to a small door at the back of the shop. "You don't even need to ask."

Solidad's office was barely a closet, but Elisabeth and Faye managed to squeeze inside, with Faye sitting in the chair behind the desk and Elisabeth in a metal folding chair she found propped against the wall. Liam stood inside the doorway with the door ajar, watching the shop and the street outside the front windows.

"You spoke to my mother?" Faye's fingers massaged her knuckles.

It occurred to Elisabeth that she ought to reassure her

that they had indeed met Mrs. Torres, so she reached into her laptop case and pulled out the small plastic container of *paciencia* cookies that Faye's mom had given to her.

Faye's eyes lit up, then filled with tears as she saw the cookies. "I was supposed to come help her make cookies this weekend."

"We went to see her because she helped Joslyn on her way north to Sonoma," Elisabeth said.

"Did Joslyn make it to Wings?"

"Yes. That's where I met her. But she was so afraid of Tomas that she took off in the middle of the night."

"You saw her? He really hurt her."

Elisabeth nodded. "Tomas came to Sonoma looking for her. He found out I helped her and now he's after me."

Faye grew white. "Oh, no."

"Faye," Elisabeth said gently, "we're looking for evidence that can put Tomas away for your uncle's murder. Then Joslyn will be safe."

Faye began to tremble violently. "You don't understand. It's not just the murder. It involves the Tumibays, too."

"How does it involve them? Why are they after you?"

The girl took a deep breath and she began to cry again. "My boyfriend—Daniel—said he'd help Joslyn. He knew her boyfriend was a Bagsic captain because *I* told him when I found out a month or two ago." She squeezed her eyes shut, and the tears trickled down her cheeks. "I thought Daniel would offer Joslyn protection from Tomas because she'd obviously broken any Bagsic ties."

"So you took Joslyn to Daniel?" Liam's voice was gentle, nonjudgmental.

Faye let out a sob. "They tied her up in the back room of their club—it's just a warehouse where they hold raves—and they threatened to kill her if she didn't give them some useful information about the Bagsics. It's my fault." The sobs were coming hard now, and Faye had difficulty speaking. "I begged her to give them something. I was so afraid they'd kill her."

Elisabeth reached out to clasp Faye's hand.

"So…she told them about the Bagsics' next ephedrine shipment from the Philippines. Joslyn had overheard Tomas talking about it with one of the other captains because he was in charge of the shipment. Then I heard Daniel planning with the other Tumibays to steal it." Faye looked at Elisabeth and Liam with wide eyes. "I knew Tomas would kill Joslyn for telling the Tumibays. I also started to suspect that Daniel might use Joslyn as leverage and offer her to Tomas in trade for something. So I helped her escape. There was a rave at the warehouse that night, so it was easy to sneak her out. She looked like any of the other girls there."

"That was pretty brave of you," Liam said.

"Not really. I thought no one knew about it. But then about a week ago, one of the girls who was at the rave that night mentioned to Daniel that she'd seen me with Joslyn. Daniel came after me. I was at a coffee shop and he tried to grab me, but I got away from him. I went home to pack a bag, I got my paycheck at work, and I've been hiding out, staying at hotels." Her shoulders heaved. "I knew I couldn't live like that forever, but I didn't know what to do."

"We'll take you somewhere safe, where the Tumibays can't get to you."

Faye gulped in a breath. "Really? Oh, thank you." The relief seemed to pour off her in waves.

"Faye." Liam went and crouched down beside her chair. "What do you remember about that shipping container?"

"Um…it was off the *Pansit*. It was due to arrive the day after they captured Joslyn, so that's two days after her dad was killed. She told them the number of the container, but I don't remember it. I'm sorry."

"Don't be sorry. Is there anything else you can tell us about it, or what the Tumibays did?"

"They made some sort of plan to transport it by truck up from the Port of Los Angeles to the Bay Area. About a week after they'd taken the shipping container, I overheard Daniel saying it was safe to keep it at 'Norris' indefinitely because no one knew the company was connected to the Tumibays. I think he was talking about IRF Norris, a pharmaceutical company. If what he said is true, then the container is still there."

Elisabeth's breath hitched. She met Liam's gaze and knew they were both thinking the same thing.

She turned to Faye. "We're going to take you somewhere safe. The Tumibays are still looking for you."

"Let me say goodbye to Solidad. She's been so helpful to me."

While Faye was with her friend, Liam and Elisabeth talked in low voices several feet away.

"So Tomas lost a shipment of ephedrine from the Philippines," Elisabeth said. "I should have guessed this all had something to do with the Bagsics' meth dealing."

"And the Tumibays stole it after they forced Joslyn to tell them about it." Liam blew out a long breath. "No wonder Tomas wants Joslyn so badly. He can't let her get away with spilling Bagsic secrets. Tomas's bosses must be livid."

"And like Faye said, the Tumibays probably want Joslyn as leverage against the Bagsics."

"But this simplifies things," Liam said. "If we find that Bagsic shipping container on the property of a Tumibay-owned company, we can give that information to the FBI. They can eliminate the Bagsics' ephedrine supplier in the Philippines—just like they did to the Tumibays a few months ago—and put some heat on the Tumibays for possessing the container."

"If Tomas hadn't murdered Felix Dimalanta, none of

this would have happened." Elisabeth watched Faye hugging Solidad.

"Shall we take her to Wings shelter?" Liam said.

"That's what I was thinking."

Liam captured her with his dark blue eyes, brilliant like sapphires, intense with a fire of determination. "And then we pay a visit to IRF Norris."

Liam and Elisabeth crouched in the bushes bordering the edge of the business complex in Marin. With the darkness of night, the temperature had dropped dramatically, and even with gloves on, his hands were cold. They had to be careful, or else the condensation from their breath would give them away.

IRF Norris. Liam had done the internet research and discovered it was a Nevada-based pharmaceutical company, but with a laboratory here in Marin, just across the bridge from San Francisco.

They'd taken Faye to Wings shelter in Sonoma, with its newly repaired front door and new security guard to replace Bill while he recovered from his injuries. They'd also informed Wings and Detective Carter about the threat to Faye's life, and Faye had been reassured that the Tumibays would not be able to get to her even if they found her.

But to eliminate the threat to her, and to Joslyn and Elisabeth, and Liam's family, they needed to find the shipping container here, tonight. Everything hinged on what they'd find.

They'd arrived about twenty minutes ago, and the building was quiet. Almost…deserted. It was the only building on this corner of the business complex, surrounded on three sides by grassy lawn, cement walkways and lots of lampposts.

They'd already scoped out the layout and knew that the only way to get to the shipping-and-receiving bay was to cross open lawn and then move around the corner of the building. In full view of anyone watching.

"So do we run for it, or walk and pretend like we're supposed to be here?" Elisabeth asked.

"I haven't seen any campus security guards, but I've seen one or two cameras," Liam said.

"They could be only for show. I think that camera there has its cable cut—you can just see it under the lens. And the building is looking rather shabby. Maybe they can't afford closed-circuit video."

"Then let's go for it—as fast as we can. The less time we're out in the open, the better."

They took off at a full sprint down the gently rolling lawn, across a cement walkway and turning down another. Then Elisabeth slowed. "Liam, wait."

"What?" The lampposts left them completely exposed.

"Look." She had paused next to an office window.

Most of the windows had closed blinds but this one had a crack through the strips. And inside there was a large area, which would be used for cubicles, except it was entirely empty with only bits of trash on the scuffed carpet.

"This is supposed to be a lab," he said. "So where's the lab?"

"Back there, I looked through another window and the room inside was empty, too."

"Maybe the labs are on the other floors. Come on, let's go."

They turned the corner and came to the shipping-and-receiving bay. It had its own driveway to separate it from the building's parking lot, but there were no light posts or floodlights. The entire bay was in darkness.

Liam switched on the flashlight he'd brought with him and immediately saw the dark blue shipping container. It was still on the wheeled trailer from the truck that had transported it. "Let's get the number down and get out—"

Car headlights flashed, illuminating the back wall of the receiving bay.

"Over here!" Elisabeth darted under the shipping container trailer and crouched behind one of the large wheels.

Liam followed not a moment too soon. A car coasted up the driveway to the receiving bay, parking only a few feet away from where they were hidden. Liam pressed his back to the cement of the docking bay wall, his heart slamming in his chest.

Two car doors opened and slammed shut. The two men who emerged continued a conversation they'd been having.

"Daniel is overreacting."

"Well, Sonny ID'd them at Faye's apartment."

"But even if they find Faye, it's not like she knows about this place."

"Daniel's just trying to cover his butt. He's in the doghouse because he let Faye get away."

The men were talking about Liam and Elisabeth and Faye.

"So where's the truck? I don't want to be here all night."

"It'll be here soon."

Panic tightened Liam's chest muscles. The Tumibays were going to move the shipping container. Even if Liam and Elisabeth got the container number and the address of this building to the FBI, if the container wasn't here, on this property, there would be no proof of ties to the Tumibays.

"Can we slash the trailer tires?" Elisabeth whispered to him. It was exactly what he had been wondering.

He tried to think about the specialty tires on the larger trucks he'd used. "I don't think so. These big tires are at high pressure and I'm not sure if they'd explode or not."

"When that truck comes to hook up to this trailer, they'll see us. We have to get out of here before then."

The frustration welled up inside him. They were so

close! But he didn't want to think what would happen if the Tumibays captured Elisabeth. "Okay, let's get the number and go."

"I already memorized it from earlier."

They'd be exposed once they ran out from behind the tires, but if they moved quickly and quietly, they could cut around the side wall and out of sight.

"Go," he mouthed to her, and she darted along the wall, her footsteps soft shushing sounds against the asphalt. The men continued talking. Liam took a deep breath, then ran for it.

He'd just turned the corner and out of sight when he heard one of the men say, "What was that?"

"What was what?"

Liam and Elisabeth were still horribly exposed by the outside lights as they made their way around the other side of the building. But once they reached the far corner, they stopped. There was about five hundred feet of lawn in front of them before they could make it to the cover of the trees. The problem was that with the angle, the men standing by the car could easily see them as soon as they got onto the grass.

"There's no help for it." Liam paused, then pulled out his firearm.

Elisabeth took a few short, hard breaths. "Okay." Her gun appeared in her hand.

"Go."

They sprinted, and almost immediately, they heard a man yell, "Hey! It's them!" Within seconds, the report of a gun echoed from the walls of the building, climbing the rolling lawn after Liam. Elisabeth ducked, maybe instinctively, and returned fire while she kept running.

His chest felt as if it had caved in. He staggered. The cold air was suddenly hot and arid. Dust was in his nose. The gunfire was suddenly rapid-fire in his ears.

"Liam, come on!" He heard her voice in his ear, her hand yanking at his shoulder. He stumbled as best as he could. His legs wouldn't respond to him.

Then he was on the ground, breathing in sand and dirt, smelling scrub brush and gunpowder and blood. And at the same time he smelled cold grass and wet earth. The gunfire tattooed over his head.

"Liam."

Elisabeth shook him violently, and the sand receded. His arm felt bruised. She must have shaken him hard in order to get him out of his mind.

"We have to go." She twisted to return fire around the edge of the stand of fir trees where they had taken cover.

He dug his fingers into the dirt, feeling the cold and wet in order to drag himself out of the vestiges of the hallucination still on the edges of his vision. "Okay. Let's go."

She peppered the men with a round of gunfire, then grabbed Liam under his arm and they ran toward where their car was parked alongside the curb.

The next thing he knew, they were driving on the road that led from the business complex. His heart beat fast and heavy in his throat, and he panted.

"You're okay," she said to him. "Focus on your breathing. You're okay."

He wasn't okay.

Things were getting worse, not better. He'd stopped his counseling because it hadn't seemed to be doing anything, but the events of the past few days made him feel like he was going crazy. He had to find a way to keep it together or he'd keep putting people in danger.

He was disgusted with himself.

"Liam."

He felt her touch on his hand as she spoke.

He was tainted. He was flawed. He'd been feeling attraction for Elisabeth, but tonight only reiterated how broken he was. He pulled his hand away from her.

"Liam, you're okay."

"I will be." His voice was rough.

"Did you want to—"

"No."

He didn't look at her. He couldn't bear to see pity or worry in her eyes. He'd done enough to burden the people around him. He needed to find a way to handle this himself.

Had they really accomplished anything from tonight? They could give the shipping container number to the FBI, who could probably track down the Bagsics' ephedrine supplier in the Philippines.

But within the hour, the Tumibays would move the shipping container from this facility. There would be no provable connection to the San Francisco gang.

The Tumibays knew that Liam and Elisabeth had seen the container. And the Tumibays would do everything they could to silence them.

He heard a faint buzzing, and Elisabeth frowned. She pulled her cell phone out of her jacket pocket. "I've got a voice mail from my answering service."

She pulled onto the side of the road and checked her voice mail. Liam concentrated on his heart rate and his breathing. His hands and legs were still trembling as if from the aftereffects of shock.

"Oh, my," Elisabeth breathed.

Her face was so pale that he grabbed her arm. "What is it? What's wrong?"

Her mouth hung open, and she blinked at her cell phone in shock. Finally she swallowed. "I just had a message... from Joslyn. It was really her, I could tell it was her voice. She said...Tomas has found her."

THIRTEEN

The sound of Joslyn's voice had ripped into Elisabeth's chest. The only reason Joslyn would be contacting her would be because something was dangerously wrong.

"What did she say?" Liam's eyes were still hollow and his face gaunt. She'd known he'd been fighting his anxiety and hallucinations as soon as she looked back and saw him stumble. All she'd been able to think of was to get him under cover and find some way to help him.

"She left a phone number for me to call."

"Don't use your phone. I have a burner." Liam hesitated, as if gathering his thoughts. "It's in my laptop case." He twisted around to grab it from the backseat and handed it to her. He was recovering quickly, but he still looked haunted.

She called the number Joslyn had given. It rang once, twice, three times. Then Joslyn's timid voice. "Hello?"

"Joslyn, it's Elisabeth."

"Thank You, God." Joslyn sobbed once, then Elisabeth heard her inhale. "I was praying you'd get my message quickly."

Elisabeth wasn't sure what God had to do with it, but this wasn't the time for that question. "Joslyn, I have to ask this. What was I wearing when we first met?"

Her heartbeat sped up at the length of time Joslyn remained silent. Was this Joslyn or just another impostor who had somehow gotten Elisabeth's answering service number?

Finally Joslyn said, "That 'Candy Crush' T-shirt. I told you I was addicted to that game."

Elisabeth let out a breath. "I'm sorry, I had to be sure. Did you call the shelter yesterday and leave a message for me?"

"No." Joslyn's voice was wary. "Someone called the shelter and said she was me?"

"Whoever it was didn't leave a phone number or say where she was, just asked me to come get her. That's why I suspected it wasn't you, because you never told me where you were going."

"Oh, Elisabeth." Joslyn took a quick breath. "It must have been someone connected to Tomas."

"I know about the Bagsics, and the Tumibays. I spoke to Faye."

"Is she all right?"

"She's fine. I took her to Wings. The Tumibays don't know where she is."

"We're in so much danger." Joslyn swallowed. "I was in Oregon, in a little town called Mattsonville. I found a job as an admin at a sheep-and-wool farm near the California border. Mattsonville is really small, so people noticed when Filipino men claiming to be my cousins came looking for me. Then I saw Tomas in town. I don't know if he saw me, but I packed my things and ran. I caught a ride with a neighboring farmer who makes deliveries along the coast."

"I'll come and get you. Where are you?"

"Penny Bay. I'm calling from the pay phone near the grocery store."

"Get a burner cell phone," Elisabeth said. "Phone my answering service and leave your number. Then find somewhere to hide. I'll be there in a few hours."

"Please hurry," she whispered, and hung up.

"I don't know how, but the Bagsics found Joslyn," Elisabeth told Liam.

Liam groaned. "They must have hired another skip tracer."

"There's nothing we could have done about it. Right now we need to find a way to get to Joslyn without the Bagsics or the Tumibays following us."

Liam's brow furrowed. "I might have an idea. Let me call Nathan."

Despite the late hour, Nathan answered Liam's call. "He said to come over," Liam said after he hung up.

"Do you think the Tumibays might be watching Nathan's home as they did with your family?" Elisabeth drove back onto the road and headed for the highway.

Liam was silent. "I'm not sure. But just in case, let's go the back way."

Once they were nearing Sonoma, Liam directed her to lonely country roads and winding lanes, and even across a couple fields. They parked in a cul-de-sac of a small housing community, and then walked through a playground and across the corner of a vineyard to emerge at the corner of Nathan's backyard.

Nathan met them at his back door. "Took you long enough to get here."

"If you'd taken any longer, I was going to eat your dinner." Shaun O'Neill rose from Nathan's kitchen table. Brady also got to his feet as Liam and Elisabeth entered the house.

Liam looked less than pleased. "What are you doing here? It's too dangerous—"

"Oh, don't be a mother hen." Despite Liam's stiff shoulders, Shaun wrapped his arms around his brother and gave a bone-creaking squeeze that had Liam grunting.

Liam glared at him, but then Brady came up behind him

with a hug almost as tight, hampered only by his injury. "You two are going to kill me," Liam muttered.

"No, we're going to save your bacon by helping you, even when you're too boneheaded to ask," Shaun said.

"What about Dad? Monica? Debra and Ryan—"

"Detective Carter is at Dad's house right now, enjoying Monica's cooking." Brady nodded to the kitchen table. "She sent food for you two, also. Nice to see you in one piece, Elisabeth." Brady smiled, looking so much like Shaun, and then he folded her in an embrace.

She jerked in surprise, but his hug was warm, encompassing. As if she was an adopted sister, to be treated like one of them.

"My turn." Shaun muscled his brother over and also gave her a hug. "We were praying for you guys," he murmured in her ear, his voice low.

A warmth pooled under her breastbone, making it hard for her to breathe. Liam's family was affecting her in ways no one else ever had. They were restoring her belief in good people. They made her feel as if she belonged.

"Let's eat." Nathan rubbed his hands together. "We've been waiting for you two to get here."

"Please tell me you two weren't followed here," Liam said.

"Of course not," Shaun said. "I was driving."

"My car," Brady said, shooting Shaun a baleful look. "He almost got into three accidents and he warped my alignment."

Liam smiled, and some of the deadness, which had been there since the shoot-out at the pharmaceutical company, dissolved from his eyes. "That's your fault. You're the only one of us who lets Shaun drive your car."

"I wouldn't want to drive your piece of junk," Shaun said to Liam. "Your sorry excuse for a truck is more likely to blow up in my face."

Elisabeth sat at the table. "By all means, keep arguing. I'll just finish the enchiladas by myself."

The men hopped into chairs with alacrity, and Elisabeth smiled at how much like little boys they could be. Nathan had already set out plates and utensils.

Then Nathan said, "I'll bless the food," and bowed his head. The O'Neills followed suit.

Elisabeth also bowed her head. She expected to feel awkward, as she usually did when Christians prayed before a meal, but somehow Nathan's words were like a balm over her soul. How strange to be thanking God for a meal when a couple hours ago she'd been dodging bullets. And yet maybe, just maybe, none of those bullets had hit them because of some divine intervention?

The O'Neills and their friend Nathan were some of the most genuine people she'd ever met. Was it their faith that made them that way?

Her wandering thoughts were brought back to the food when Nathan said, "Amen." Then she had to almost fight for her share as the boys tackled the baking dish of shredded chicken enchiladas.

"So tell us what happened," Shaun said.

Elisabeth and Liam told them everything they knew about the Bagsics and Tumibays, and then about Joslyn's call.

"I have an idea," Brady said. "You can borrow my friend's car."

"Doesn't he need it?" Liam asked.

"He's on vacation, and he won't mind, I promise." Brady fished out his key ring from his pocket. "He gave me the key in case I needed to use it. It's parked in a parking garage just outside downtown Sonoma."

"That way, the Bagsics won't recognize your car," Shaun said. "As for disguises…"

Liam shook his head. "They already know our faces. We'll wear hats and hope for the best."

"You've got to tell the FBI about the shipping container, even though the Tumibays have already moved it by now," Shaun said. "Monica's cousin was involved in something this past spring that let the FBI crack down on the Tumibays' ephedrine supplier in the Philippines. They could do the same with the Bagsics' supplier."

"I called them while we were driving back to Sonoma," Elisabeth said. "They were hopeful and promised to look into it."

"There might be enough evidence to put Tomas away for good," Nathan said. "And not just Tomas, but maybe even the entire Bagsic gang."

The talk eventually turned to their personal lives—how Patrick O'Neill was responding to chemotherapy for his leukemia, Shaun's job as head of security for the Joy Luck Life Hotel and Spa and Nathan's upcoming wedding. They joked about the loud Christmas parties they had now that Monica's family and Nathan's were included.

Elisabeth had never been huge on Christmas parties. The ones at Wings were always a bit sad because the women were missing their families and recovering from the pain and betrayal they'd experienced. Before she'd become a private investigator, her friends had been a wild bunch, preferring parties involving lots of alcohol to Christmas dinners and friendly gatherings.

She'd never particularly desired that picture-perfect Christmas before, but listening to the O'Neills and Nathan, she felt the loneliness like a cold, icy puddle in her heart. She didn't have anyone to share the holiday with.

Hadn't she wanted it that way? When she let people in, they had hurt her.

But somehow, she couldn't convince herself that the O'Neills would hurt her.

When Liam yawned, Nathan started clearing away the dishes. "You two are staying here tonight."

"No, Nathan—"

"I'm perfectly capable of tying you to my guest bed, Liam."

"I'll help." Shaun gave a wicked grin.

"But the gangs…" Elisabeth began.

Nathan laid a gentle hand on her shoulder. "You two are exhausted. My home has extra bedrooms and a great alarm system. And it's only for a few short hours. You can't help Joslyn if you're both burned to the socket."

Her eyes did feel gritty and tight. "Thanks," she said awkwardly.

"You are exactly like Liam," Shaun said. "You both hate receiving help from people."

"Not true." Liam paused as he gave a gigantic yawn. "I would have loved help cleaning my room when we were kids, but I got used to you guys abandoning me in my hour of need."

"You're really going to blame it on that?" Brady rolled his eyes. "Liam, you had intelligent life growing out of the science experiment otherwise known as the underside of your bed."

"You always were squeamish." Shaun nudged Brady with his foot.

His brothers' teasing had brought the light back into Liam's blue eyes. And Elisabeth realized how relieved she was to see it there.

Back at the pharmaceutical company, she'd been focused on keeping him alive and sane. And now she wanted to help him heal the rift in his mind.

She had the same type of focus when she encountered a woman in need at the shelter. She put all her energies into fulfilling needs, whether they were emotional or practical. She was a shoulder to cry on, a sounding board, a voice of reason. She used her skills to train women and help them start new lives.

She felt that same desire to help Liam. He'd come to mean a great deal to her. She respected him. He was different from other people in her life.

And she realized, with both elation and dread, that she might be coming to trust him. She hadn't trusted anyone in a long time, but there was something about Liam, his intelligence, his abilities and his family—and yes, even his quiet faith—that made her want to trust him.

And that frightened her more than bullets, more than the two gangs after her.

"We're being followed. Black SUV."

At Liam's words, Elisabeth checked her rearview mirror. "How? Did they follow us from Nathan's house?"

"Maybe. All I know is that they're not Bagsics," Liam said. "It's not a four-car team, and they're not nearly as good."

They were on their way to pick up Brady's friend's car, the morning light barely turning the buildings of downtown Sonoma a pearly peach color. "We can't go to the parking garage while they're behind us."

"Oh, no." Liam adjusted the passenger-side mirror. "I think there's two cars."

"What's the second car?"

"Silver Camaro."

She looked back and saw it. "I'm going to try to lose them."

"No, wait. Head out of town. I have an idea."

Liam directed her to a residential area outside of town, just before the lots opened up to farms and vineyards. "Once you turn this corner, turn again right away and then stop and let me out."

"What?"

"It'll split up the tail. You lose one car, I'll lose the other."

"On foot?" But Elisabeth turned as he had instructed.

"I know Sonoma like the back of my hand. I can run through alleys and parking lots to lose him." He unbuckled his seat belt.

She turned again and came to a jerking halt, but Liam was out the door even before the car stopped. "I'll meet you at the parking garage." He was out of sight between two houses before she could blink.

She darted forward and took the next left just as she saw a black SUV turn onto the street behind her.

She took advantage of the twisted streets of the residential area to put some distance between herself and the SUV. They knew by now she was onto them, but that wasn't important. They couldn't do anything except try to keep her in sight.

She turned onto a busy street, cutting rather close in front of another car and causing a snag in the intersection, as well as collecting a few horn honks. But she underestimated the SUV—it muscled its way into the flow of traffic and then made some dangerous maneuvers to keep up with her.

She moved into the right-hand lane. When the SUV moved into the lane to her left, she slowed until it was directly alongside her. Two Tumibays—their wrist tattoos on full display—gave her feral grins.

She sped up. The SUV kept pace with her.

Perfect.

Without warning, she abruptly turned right down a side street. The SUV couldn't turn in time and continued going straight.

She immediately made another right turn to head back the way she'd come—and had to brake hard.

Two cars sat in the middle of the residential street, the

two drivers talking to each other. They completely blocked the road. The drivers saw her and started to end their conversation, easing away from each other inch by inch. She resisted the urge to lay on her horn, and looked in her rearview mirror in time to see the SUV turn onto the street and bear down on her.

Finally the drivers cleared away, and she swerved around the car in front of her to speed down the lane. She had to get distance between herself and the SUV.

She turned down some more streets, but there were several cars and it was dangerous for her to be passing them on these residential streets. She needed to make her followers make a colossal mistake.

She headed to the freeway entrance.

The SUV had fallen a few cars behind, so she slowed down and maneuvered to allow it to get right on her tail. The closest freeway entrance would lead her back in the direction of the parking garage, not away from it, but if her plan worked, it wouldn't matter. When she turned onto the on-ramp to the freeway, the SUV was barely a car length behind her.

The on-ramp became an exit-only lane for the next freeway exit, so she moved to the left lane. The SUV followed, cutting off a Honda Civic.

Then, just as the exit-only lane curved right and away from the freeway, she swerved right, cutting in front of a car in the lane, and exited the freeway.

The SUV had been following too close, and it was less maneuverable than her car. It had shot past the exit in the blink of an eye.

She drove on, watching behind her in case there was another car tailing her. There was a line of cars waiting to get into the parking lot of a shopping center, which was stuffed to the gills with Christmas shoppers. She got in line and circled the parking lot, but no one seemed to be following her.

Her cell phone rang, and so she stopped on the right side of the aisle, like a car waiting for someone to back out of a space. The cars behind her simply moved around her.

It was Liam. "Are you all right?" she asked.

"Yeah, I lost them. Where are you?" There was an echoing quality to his voice.

"I'm not far away in a shopping center parking lot. I was making sure I didn't have another car following me."

"I'm at the parking garage. I found the car." That explained the echo.

"I'll be there in a few minutes," she said.

"Okay. Bye."

She was about to disconnect the call when she suddenly heard a commotion in the background of Liam's phone, a scuffling, then a clattering, which she thought was the phone landing on the ground. The muffled sounds that might be punches. Then the sharp "Oof!" of Liam grunting.

And then a lone footstep. A shoe with a heel that clicked when it struck the ground, not the sneakers Liam had been wearing.

Elisabeth disconnected the call immediately, her heart slamming in her chest. If that had been Liam being knocked out by someone, she couldn't have them knowing that she'd heard the fight.

She couldn't breathe, although she was gasping. Her chest hurt. The edges of her vision started to cloud in on her.

Get hold of yourself! She gripped the steering wheel, forced her diaphragm out, then in. Air rushed into her lungs. The dizziness passed and her head cleared, bringing back her sense of resolve. She had to do something to help Liam.

She put the car in gear and got out of the parking lot as fast as possible. She sped down the road, figuring out the fastest way to the parking garage. She couldn't think about the SUV following her now. She had to get to Liam before anything worse happened to him. If whoever had fought with him took him away from the garage, she'd never find him.

She checked her phone. If Liam was all right, he'd have called her to tell her what happened, but there was no call.

She couldn't fool herself anymore. Liam had come to mean a lot more to her than she wanted him to. She had to save him. He had to be all right.

Oh, God, please help me! Even as the prayer formed, she felt guilty. She hadn't prayed in years, since her mother took her to Sunday school. Why would God listen to her now?

Because God was best buds with Liam.

That thought somehow calmed her, helped her think more clearly. At a stoplight, she put her phone on speaker and dialed Detective Carter.

"Hey, Elisabeth."

"Liam's been attacked."

"What?" The detective's voice sharpened. "Where?"

She gave him the address of the parking garage and where the borrowed car was parked. "Please hurry."

The light turned green and she disconnected the call and shot forward. Within a minute, she was in sight of the garage.

Then a silver Camaro caught her eye.

That had been the car that had followed Liam. It was parked a couple blocks away from the parking garage. Liam had said he'd lost the car tailing him, which would be easy to do if he took shortcuts and alleyways, going places the car couldn't follow.

But once the Camaro lost Liam, it must have doubled

back. Maybe its driver had guessed at what point Elisabeth had realized they were being followed. It would make sense that up until that point, she had been heading somewhere specific, and that Liam would make his way back in that direction eventually.

If the Camaro belonged to the Tumibay who'd followed Liam, that meant Liam was still at the parking garage. Elisabeth had the keys to the borrowed car in her purse. The Tumibay hadn't taken Liam away.

She pulled alongside the street and parallel parked. Remembering her idea for the shipping container's trailer, she looked in a toolbox in her trunk for her needle-nose pliers, then went to the Camaro's tires. She removed the valve cap and used the pliers to unscrew the valve cores entirely. Air whooshed from each tire as she worked her way around the car.

Elisabeth had to take a moment to catch her breath as the panic began to well up again. No, she had to stay in control of herself. She couldn't help Liam if she lost it.

She hadn't realized how much she'd come to depend on Liam, on his strength and abilities, on his calmness. Even his faith had had an impact on her.

She hadn't depended on anyone in a long time. She hadn't wanted to get close to someone else who would hurt her.

But Liam had sneaked under her defenses. He was dedicated to his loved ones, despite his PTSD and his shoulder injury. He wouldn't let his loved ones down. He wouldn't let *her* down.

Her fist clenched her shirt over her breastbone. She wouldn't let him down, either.

FOURTEEN

"Hey, wake up."

The sharp slap on his face snapped Liam out of darkness. He tried to open his eyes and immediately regretted it as light made pain radiate from his temple. It felt as though his skull had been smashed in. He groaned and turned onto his side.

Liam had heard the man coming up behind him a footstep too late. By the time he'd realized someone was there, the attacker was too close. Liam had tried to strike out, but the blows had only glanced off the man's shoulder and ear. Then the man had swung hard and the lights went out.

There was a hard kick to his shin. "Get up," a man growled.

He opened his eyes and saw his cell phone on the ground, underneath the car. Elisabeth. He'd been talking to her. She'd have no idea what had happened to him.

And she was coming here now.

Another kick, harder this time. "I said, get up."

His running had made him slow and tired, but he shouldn't have let down his guard like that. He'd just put Elisabeth in danger. Again.

He wasn't going to let anything happen to her.

He got onto his hands and knees, and a wave of nausea clenched his stomach. Tiny bits of gravel bit into his palms, and he concentrated on the slight pain to keep himself from getting sick all over the cement ground.

"Come on, I ain't going to carry you."

So that was why he'd woken Liam up. He had seen Liam at the car and probably guessed he would be using it, but he couldn't get into the borrowed car without setting off the alarm, and Liam didn't have the car keys. He'd have to transport them with his car, which was probably not in the garage. Liam got into a sitting position, leaning against the car tire.

It was the same man from the gas station who had held Elisabeth at gunpoint, and who had been at Brady's house, the one with the fishhook-shaped scar on his face. Lamar Garcia. He looked a little worse for wear with a purple bruise over one eye and over his cheek. But his hand holding the gun was steady as he pointed it at Liam.

"Get up," he ordered.

"You were at the gas station."

"Yeah, I've seen enough of you the past couple days to last me a lifetime. Your brother's house is nice, by the way." He gave a snakelike smile.

"Nice shiner." Which was probably what Liam had given to him when he'd tackled the man.

Garcia's smile flattened. "Stand up. We're going to take a ride." Liam started to get up when the man added, "Oh, and toss me your cell phone."

Liam slowly retrieved the phone from under the car, then threw it to the man's feet. He frowned at Liam, but kept the gun pointed at him as he bent to pick it up.

"You were on the phone with her, I'm guessing. I heard you while I was sneaking up on you." He chuckled. "Didn't think that would be so easy."

"Yes, you're very smart," Liam said drily.

"She's coming here, isn't she?"

Liam stilled.

"Let's roll out the welcome wagon." Keeping his eyes and gun on Liam, Garcia pocketed Liam's phone and pulled out his own. His eyes flickered from his phone to Liam as he dialed.

Liam considered attacking, but he was still dizzy and didn't like his chances against the man's trigger finger. There had to be something he could do to protect Elisabeth, but his pounding head made it hard to think. Fear began to build in his chest. What could he do?

Cast adrift, he mentally reached out for something to cling to and hit on the calm certainty of his faith. He wasn't truly alone, he reminded himself. God was with him.

His worry and fear receded, but he still couldn't figure out what to do. He had to do something. He had to think! Elisabeth depended on him.

The Tumibay was talking into his phone. "The girl's going to come here. Parking garage on the corner of Miles Street and City Avenue. Get here fast." He disconnected the call, then jerked his gun at Liam. "Walk."

Liam's legs were leaden, and he had to strain to put one foot in front of the other. He stumbled toward the stairs to the parking garage and hung on to the railing as he walked down. He started regaining his strength but kept his movements clumsy.

They headed down the deserted sidewalk. "Why do you want Joslyn?" he asked, figuring he might as well make the most of this chance to gain new intel.

"The Bagsics want to kill her," Garcia replied, "which means they'd be willing to pay to have her." The man's confidence was making him chatty.

"They won't pay you for her. If you have her, they'll come after you."

Garcia laughed. "We can handle them. Keep going." They went another block, then the man said, "Stop here."

Liam recognized the silver Camaro. The Tumibay

pulled his keys out of his pocket and clicked the fob. The car unlocked and the trunk popped open.

Liam didn't have much time. "Capturing us won't do you any good. When Joslyn left the shelter, she didn't tell anyone where she was going."

"Sure she didn't."

Liam gave him a sidelong look. "Why don't you ask Faye? Shouldn't she know where her own cousin went?"

The thug used the butt of his pistol to hit him, the metal crunching into his cheekbone. The pain was like an iron spike hit straight into his skull, and metallic warmth spurted over his teeth.

"Don't get smart with me."

Liam bent over and spit out blood. That was when he noticed the tires. He wiped his mouth. "You've got a flat."

"Yeah, right." Garcia moved to get a better look. "Hey!" He bent over to look at the tire. Then he turned toward the back tire and saw that it was flat, also. "My rims—!"

Liam knocked his gun away and it clattered on the sidewalk. Then he jumped him, and the two of them rolled to the sidewalk.

The blows to his face had made Liam too dizzy, and he was too slow to block a punch from the man that connected with his ear. Ringing exploded in his head.

"Hold it!"

Elisabeth.

She stood several yards away, her gun in her hands. Her hands were steady, but Liam could see the intensity of her eyes. She walked forward a couple paces and kicked the Tumibay's gun farther away.

"Get up," Elisabeth said.

Garcia slowly stood with hands raised. "Don't shoot. I wasn't going to hurt him."

"You can tell that to the police. I already called them."

The man paled, making his fishhook scar stand out

against his temple. Liam rolled over and sat up, but he had to pause to catch his breath before trying to stand.

"Look, he needs help." Garcia gestured to Liam.

"You're such a Good Samaritan." Liam wiped his mouth with his shirt, but the bleeding had stopped.

Sirens sounded in the distance. The man suddenly turned and ran.

Then Elisabeth was crouching next to him. "Oh, my, your face…" She was close enough that he could smell oranges and tuberoses.

"I'm fine." He looked into her eyes. Their gazes held a long moment.

Then she leaned forward and softly pressed her lips to his.

Elisabeth didn't know exactly why she kissed him. She'd been so relieved to see him safe, she hadn't thought about her actions. She'd simply wanted to be close to him.

When her lips touched his, something clicked. It was as if she'd been completed. It wasn't just how it felt to be kissing him, it was how he was always looking out for her, how he valued her abilities, how he made her feel special. When he looked at her, in his eyes were both admiration and honor.

No man had ever looked at her like that.

But look at how the other men in her life had treated her. Hadn't she chosen to be alone because she couldn't pick up the pieces of her life again a third time? She wouldn't be able to.

And certainly not after Liam.

She leaned back. She met his eyes for a brief moment, then looked away. She wouldn't be mesmerized by his eyes again.

Elisabeth rose to her feet as the sirens grew screamingly close. She ran to Officer Joseph Fong. "The man who attacked Liam ran that way. His name is Lamar Garcia. Black jacket, jeans, fishhook scar on his left cheekbone."

He took off on foot down the alley. She was glad the police were here, but they were a minute too late. "I should have gone after him," she muttered.

"No, you shouldn't," Liam said, still sitting on the ground. "You don't know if he'd have led you straight to his friends."

She hadn't thought of that.

"They were supposed to meet him here, but they might have taken off when they saw the squad car." Liam got to his feet, his knees shaky. His face went white for a brief moment, and he closed his eyes.

"Liam." She went to him to grab him if he fainted.

Some color came back into his cheeks. He opened his eyes. She was about to step back when his hands came up to frame her face. His touch was like a whisk to her brain. She couldn't hold a coherent thought.

"How did you know?" he asked.

"Know what?"

"That I was in trouble."

"Oh." She blinked, remembering. "I didn't disconnect the call right away, and so I heard you struggling with him. And then I heard only one footstep, and it wasn't yours."

He stared at her. "You just happened to hear it all?"

His expression made her realize for the first time how odd it had been that she hadn't hung up right away, that she'd heard everything. "It was such a freak thing."

He shook his head, and his eyes were serious, and wondering, and reverent. "I think it was God," he breathed. "I think He saved me."

With his hands cupping her face, she had a hard time objecting to his words, especially because she knew she couldn't explain the coincidence.

By that time, a second squad car had pulled up and the officer approached. "Are you both all right?"

"He'll need—"

The officer interrupted her. "I've called the paramedics."

At that moment, Officer Fong appeared, breathing heavily. "I don't know where he went. Sorry, folks."

Liam clearly chafed at the delay as he submitted to being patched up by the paramedics and gave his statement to Officer Fong. However, neither Elisabeth nor Liam mentioned Joslyn or the reason they were at the parking lot.

Detective Carter arrived, and soon after, Shaun and Monica. Liam's brother looked grave and even a little dangerous, and Monica gave her husband worried looks as she hurried alongside him.

"How did they find you?" Shaun said.

"We're not sure," Elisabeth said.

She recounted everything to Detective Carter, who sighed when she finished. "That's it. You two are coming to the station with me. You're getting an officer to protect you—"

"We can't." Elisabeth lowered her voice. "Joslyn is in danger."

The detective frowned. "I can send an officer—"

"She won't go with him."

He sighed again, closing his eyes and massaging his forehead with his fingers. Then he said, "You've given your statements?"

"Yes, sir."

"Then go." Detective Carter stomped away, clearly unhappy.

"At least he didn't arrest you," Shaun said cheerfully. "He looked mad enough that he might have, just to keep you out of trouble."

Monica smiled. "He arrested my sister once, and my

aunt laid into him. He's just worried about you two. He called us right after you called him."

"The Tumibay saw the borrowed car," Liam said. "I was standing at the driver's-side door when he attacked me. We shouldn't use it."

Shaun nodded. "Brady guessed that when he heard where you were attacked. He had an idea. We're going to meet him."

He gave them the address and Liam and Elisabeth left first in her car, while Shaun and Monica hung back. They'd follow after a few minutes just to make sure they weren't followed. Elisabeth was grateful for the precaution, but she still watched for a tail. It was odd to have these strangers be so concerned for her. No, they were probably just concerned for Liam.

She was surprised to turn into a used car dealership and see Brady talking to a salesman. The dealership wasn't very reputable looking, which might have been why Brady chose it.

When Brady saw Liam carefully lever himself out of Elisabeth's car, his brows drew down over his eyes and he looked as fierce as Shaun had when he'd arrived at the parking garage. "You all right?"

Liam waved away his brother's concern. "It looks worse than—"

"Don't lie to me." Then Brady grinned. "You're such a baby when it comes to pain."

"I'll show you pain." Liam grabbed his brother in a headlock.

Elisabeth exchanged long-suffering looks with the car dealer, a tall, wiry man with short blond hair and a large nose. "Anytime you gents are ready…" he said with a faint British accent.

Shaun and Monica drove into the lot a few minutes later,

and Shaun, Liam and Brady began talking to the car dealer in earnest. Monica and Elisabeth stood a few feet away.

"Is Brady really going to buy a used car just for us?" Elisabeth couldn't imagine something like that.

Monica shrugged. "You two are in need. A woman's life is at stake. Besides, have you seen Liam's truck?"

Elisabeth thought back, finally recalling the beat-up pickup truck at the women's shelter. "I suppose Liam could use an upgrade."

"Liam wouldn't accept a gift from his brothers, but he would accept the help when he was in need, especially if it allowed him to help someone who was relying on him."

Yes, that sounded like Liam.

"We're glad you're all right." Monica rubbed Elisabeth's shoulder.

"I'm glad I arrived in time to help Liam." She didn't want to think what might have happened if she hadn't been able to get there so quickly. "If I hadn't overheard the attack on the phone…"

"Shaun and I have already thanked God that you did." Monica studied her brother-in-law. "Liam's been struggling a bit since he came back to Sonoma. This might help reaffirm his faith, give him some peace."

"He mentioned God, too. He said God saved him."

"You don't think so?" Monica's look was questioning.

"I don't know much about God anymore." Not since her mother had died and He'd failed her.

"It's hard to *know* God," Monica said. "There's so much we just don't understand. But faith in God can give us strength."

"How can you have faith when God doesn't always answer prayers?" Elisabeth hadn't meant to ask that, but it just came out. And she realized she really did want to know.

Monica thought a moment before answering. "I don't

know why there are some prayers He doesn't answer. I know He sees when people do awful things to each other, and I don't know why He allows that." She reached out to clasp Elisabeth's hands. "But I do know that even in the midst of suffering and pain and loneliness, He's there with us. He loves us, and we're not alone."

Monica's words had a ring of authority and confidence. She wasn't just uttering phrases to comfort herself or Elisabeth; she believed in the absolute truth of what she was saying. It was different from anything other people had said to Elisabeth before. It was as if the words had power.

Liam and his family were doing strange things to Elisabeth. She wasn't sure how she felt about it all.

"Looks like they're done haggling." Monica released Elisabeth's hands just as Liam broke away and headed toward them.

"What's the damage?" Monica asked.

"I'm paying him back." There was a stubborn set to Liam's jaw.

"Of course you are. You know that Brady's charging you interest, right?"

Liam's scowl dissolved into a smile. "It's nice of him. But don't tell him I said that."

"He wouldn't believe me if I did."

Elisabeth gave a snort of laughter.

Liam nodded at a white Mazda 4x4 pickup truck. "That's the one. Brady drove it around the block earlier. Transmission is sticky, but it'll work."

"That's a Lexus compared to your old truck," Monica said.

"Hey, it runs."

"It's an eyesore," Monica said.

Liam cleared his throat. "The Bagsics won't recognize the Mazda, and even if they checked the license plate, the dealer may not have yet submitted the notice of transfer to the DMV. And the DMV will take a while to update their records."

"I'm guessing Shaun is asking the dealer to hold off on submitting that notice of transfer?" Elisabeth asked.

"By law, he has a certain amount of time to send it in." Liam turned to Monica. "Shaun and Brady won't accept my thanks, so I'll tell you instead. Thanks for helping us out."

"We're family. Of course we'd help."

Monica said it so matter-of-factly, and again Elisabeth was struck by how the concept of a loving family came so easily to the O'Neills. What if she'd grown up differently? She'd spent so much time blaming the men in her past. Was it too late to have a different perspective?

Soon Elisabeth and Liam had transferred their things to the cab of the Mazda truck. Elisabeth drove and they headed north, with Shaun following a little ways behind them to make sure they weren't followed out of town, while Brady followed Monica in Elisabeth's car to Liam's dad's house.

A little ways past Geyserville, Shaun called Liam, who put the call on speaker. "I'll leave you two here," Shaun said. "I'd tell you two to stay out of trouble, but you were never good at that."

"Thanks," Liam said drily.

Shaun's voice was more sober as he said, "So I'll just tell you guys to stay safe."

"We will," Liam said, and disconnected the call.

"Your family is…"

"Annoying?" Liam said.

"Amazing." Elisabeth licked her lips. "You don't know how good you've got it."

"Believe me, I do." He looked steadily at her as she drove. "I'm sorry if my family bothers you."

"They don't."

"Sometimes you get a kind of look…"

Elisabeth frowned. "I hope I don't look annoyed. Because I'm not."

"No, not that. You look sad."

She bit her lip but didn't answer.

"The subject of family seems to bother you sometimes," he said. "I'm sorry if my family makes you feel worse."

She took a breath, then another. "They don't. It's me."

They were silent for a mile or two, then Liam said, "What happened to make you lose your faith in families?"

Elisabeth felt the heat rise up her neck.

"I'm sorry," Liam said immediately. "I didn't mean to be nosy."

He was always so kind, so considerate of her.

"When did your mother die?" she asked him.

He was surprised at the question, but answered, "When I was sixteen."

"Really? So did mine." She saw the cremation urn in her father's hands, the careless way he handled it. "My father got a girlfriend right away, or maybe he'd already had her when Mom was dying. His new girlfriend didn't like me very much, so one day she and Dad packed their things. Dad said the rent was paid up for the month, but they were taking off and they didn't want me tagging along. And they left."

Liam closed his eyes, his face full of pain. "I'm so sorry. I shouldn't have brought this up."

"It's all right. It's been years. And to be honest, I've met women at the shelter who have experienced much worse."

"He didn't…beat you, did he?"

"No, not at all. What made you think that?"

"I thought he was the reason you have that scar."

She touched the scar above her left cheek. Most days, she avoided mirrors and forgot about it. "No, this was from my ex-boyfriend's ring."

She saw Liam's hand clench in his lap, and strangely, his anger on her behalf made her feel…precious.

"I have no respect for men who prey on fragile people, or who take advantage of women who are alone," Liam said in a hard voice. "You were only sixteen…"

"Cruise didn't come into my life until a few years after Dad left."

"Were you in a foster home?"

"No, I was alone." At his incredulous stare, she said, "It's easier than you think. I got a job and I passed my GED. I took classes at the community college."

"You're amazing."

His words made a warmth spread across her chest. She felt as if she'd been covered by a cozy blanket. "Actually, I was selfish and self-centered, but after I landed in the hospital, some women helped me." She hadn't thought of them in years—kind women from a local church. They'd been a bit legalistic in all the rules they followed for their religion, but they'd helped her when she'd had nothing. She'd just had a hard time trusting their God after He had allowed Cruise to hurt her so much.

"Is that why you help battered women?"

"Yes. After my jaw and arm healed, I got into counseling, and my therapist helped me to heal inside. And after that, I refused to allow myself or anyone else to be a victim again." It was the reason she felt responsible for Joslyn and wanted to protect her. The gang's relentless pursuit was a form of bullying, and Elisabeth wouldn't stand for it. She wouldn't be bullied by a man again, and she wouldn't let Joslyn be bullied by them, either.

Maybe it was good she was telling Liam all this. It reminded her why she shouldn't—couldn't—put too much trust in people.

But unbidden, Monica's words came back to her:

Even in the midst of suffering and pain and loneliness, He's there with us, and He loves us, and we're not alone.

It was strange to think about God being there for her and loving her when she'd been so used to feeling isolated and unloved. Everything inside her resisted trusting Monica's claim, especially when she hadn't seen God act in her life anytime before.

She remembered that phone call, and overhearing Liam being attacked.

But that was God acting on Liam's behalf. They were best buds. God wasn't her best bud.

But what if He could be?

But why would He?

She was fine as she was. Liam made her feel special, and his family made her feel cherished, but it was only temporary. The risk wasn't worth more pain, no matter how close she and Liam had been becoming. She respected him, and she valued him, but she couldn't let him get any closer. It was better for her to be alone.

So why did that thought leave her feeling so desolate?

They drove in silence for a while, then Liam cleared his throat. "Are we going to talk about the, uh…"

The kiss. She swallowed. "I'm sorry. I was worried for you, and relieved. I wasn't thinking clearly. Maybe we should forget about it."

He was quiet a long moment. Then a bleakness and resolve came over his face. He nodded firmly. "Yes. Let's forget about it."

What was that about? But she couldn't ask when she'd just told him not to talk about it.

For a while after that, they drove in silence, but eventually they started talking about other things. Their favorite sports teams. Favorite music. Favorite books. She told him about working her way through college to get her degrees. He told her about his time in the army. He was able to speak about his shoulder injury and surgery dispassionately, but she could hear in his voice the thready pain at memories still raw.

After several hours, Liam insisted he was feeling fine enough to drive. The paramedics had cleared him, saying he didn't have a concussion, so she let him take the wheel.

They were about half an hour from Penny Bay when her cell phone rang. She recognized the number as Joslyn's burner cell. "Joslyn, we're almost—"

"He's here!" Joslyn's voice was hoarse with panic. "Somehow Tomas followed me from Mattsonville. He's here in Penny Bay!"

FIFTEEN

"Joslyn, where are you now?"

The urgency in Elisabeth's voice made Liam's pulse pound. "What's wrong?"

"Stay out of sight," Elisabeth told Joslyn. "We'll be there as fast as we can." She hung up. "Tomas is in Penny Bay."

"Wasn't he in Mattsonville? How'd he find her?"

"She doesn't know. She happened to see him on the street, so she ducked into a yarn shop."

"Will she be safe there?"

"I hope so. She says the shop is hosting its weekly knitalong, so there are a lot of women there. But Tomas and his men must be searching the town for her. She can't stay hidden for long."

"We're almost there."

Her worry was etched into her face, but she was making an effort to stay strong. He admired that about her, her caring combined with her bravery. After hearing about her father and her ex-boyfriend, he wanted to protect her from anyone else who would hurt her.

He was falling in love with her.

But the realization only felt like a knife digging into his chest. He wasn't in any shape to have a relationship with anyone, not with his nightmares and his hallucinations. He couldn't burden anyone else with what he was going through. If he found a way to heal himself, then maybe he might consider it. But until then, he was too broken.

As he took the exit to Penny Bay, he said, "If Tomas and his men see us, they'll know for sure that Joslyn is here."

"And they won't scruple to hurt other people to get what they want." Elisabeth chewed on her lip. "We need to distract them. But we can't put anyone else in danger."

"We shouldn't go directly into town, or they might spot us." Liam turned onto a bypass road rather than continuing on to Main Street.

Penny Bay sat directly on the coast, on the edge of cliffs that fell hundreds of feet into the churning winter sea. Just beyond the town was a historic lighthouse that was apparently a tourist stop.

"Wait, turn in here." Elisabeth pointed to the lighthouse entrance.

The driveway split into a wide road to the right and a narrower utility road to the left. A sign had an arrow pointing right that said Parking Lot and an arrow to the left that said Penny Bay Historic Lighthouse and Penny Bay Downtown, One Mile. No Parking This Direction. Beneath that was another sign that said Lighthouse Closed Dec-Mar.

Liam turned the car right into the mostly empty parking lot.

"Looks like there's barely anyone here to get hurt if we could lure the Bagsics there," Elisabeth said. "But I don't know how we'd do that."

"I have an idea," Liam said slowly. "But it's a little crazy."

She eyed him narrowly. "How crazy?"

"Like…backing the car into me and the Tumibay in Faye's apartment parking garage crazy."

After he told her his plan, she pursed her lips as she

thought, but finally shook her head. "Definitely crazy, but I can't come up with any other ideas."

They parked the truck and then walked down the utility road toward downtown Penny Bay. The air was frigid. The road hit a T-junction, with the utility road heading right toward the lighthouse and a footpath veering left toward the town.

They kept their heads down and headed onward, keeping their eyes peeled for any Bagsic members. They ducked into a coffee shop to avoid one who had just turned the corner to walk down the street directly toward them. They managed to head out the back way of the shop.

The small town had an eclectic collection of shops and residential homes, all decorated with cheerful Christmas lights, fir boughs and tinsel garlands. It was close to sunset, and the daylight glowed a warm orange on the weathered walls of the buildings. The town was laid out in a rough grid, and it seemed every shop had a back door that opened into an alleyway or lane.

"There's the yarn shop." Elisabeth pointed to a small building to their left.

Liam scanned around and saw an internet café down the street in the opposite direction. "That looks like a good place."

She nodded, her eyes apprehensive as they rested on him. "Be careful."

He wanted to touch her face, as he had outside the parking garage. But he couldn't do that to her. She deserved better. "You, too."

He turned down a side road until he hit Long Street, one of the main streets of the town, bordered by shops. It ran parallel to the road they'd just been on. He glued his cell phone to his ear and started shouting, "Joslyn? Is that you? I can barely hear you."

He didn't have to walk more than a block before a Bagsic noticed him. The man wasn't familiar to Liam, but he wore the distinctive purple and gray colors. Liam pretended not to see him and continued shouting into his cell phone. "Where are you? I'm here in town. Joslyn?"

Liam made his way toward the internet café and away from the yarn shop, away from Elisabeth and Joslyn. He kept shouting Joslyn's name into his cell phone to draw the attention of any other Bagsics nearby, luring them away so Elisabeth could sneak inside and bring Joslyn out without being seen. He was almost to the front door of the internet café when he glanced in the window.

Sitting beside the window was a Bagsic at a table, typing on a laptop. He had finer clothes than some of the other gang members Liam had seen, although not quite as fine as Tomas's. He seemed to be higher up the food chain, maybe just below Tomas's level or equal to it. He hadn't seen Liam and didn't even look up as Liam walked past the window. But Liam noticed the flash of metal on his wrist.

He wore a vintage Rolex watch. The same watch Liam had seen in the photos of Joslyn's father.

This man had been there when Tomas killed Felix Dimalanta. And he had stolen the man's watch.

Liam's jaw ached, and he realized he'd been clenching it. He had to stay focused or he'd never make it out of Penny Bay alive.

At the door to the internet café, he stopped and turned to face the street. From the corner of his eye, he saw the Bagsic following him duck into a souvenir shop—still within easy earshot.

"What?" Liam shouted into his phone. "You're where? The lighthouse? Okay, I'll be there in a few minutes."

He pocketed his phone and turned back the way he'd come. He didn't look into the souvenir shop and made his way quickly down the street to where it narrowed into the utility road and continued out of town to the lighthouse.

He thought he might have seen Tomas out of the corner of his eye as he passed a restaurant. By now his men would have told him what they'd overheard about Joslyn at the lighthouse, and they'd be following Liam. Hopefully at a distance.

The utility road was a straight shot that ended at the lighthouse perched on the edge of the cliffs. The road passed between two rows of historic houses converted into vacation rentals, gussied up with Christmas decorations even though it looked as though they were empty of tenants at the moment. There were one or two tourists milling around the lighthouse, but they were far down the path looking out to sea.

Liam's cell phone rang. He saw that Elisabeth had called and hung up, as they'd planned. She was in position.

He took a deep breath. He continued walking until he'd just passed the corner of a house, then he suddenly cut right and ran around the side of the building. Shouts rang out behind him.

He took another right around the backside of the house and sprinted with all his might toward the utility road. At the same time, he heard the gunning of an engine. The Mazda truck.

Elisabeth shot into view, jamming down the utility road in an intercept course with him. She turned quickly onto the grass, the truck's four-wheel drive handling the off roading with ease. She slowed as he neared her, and he took a flying leap, planting his foot on the bumper and jumping into the back of the pickup.

He landed against the metal bed, aware of Elisabeth accelerating back toward the utility road. He slid toward the tailgate, bouncing violently as the wheels jounced around on the earth. There was nothing for him to hold on to, so he just concentrated on not flying out of the truck.

Once Elisabeth reached the entrance to the highway,

she stopped. Liam climbed out of the bed. The gang members were still far down the road, running toward them.

Joslyn opened the passenger door and Liam climbed inside. "Go!" He slammed the door and fastened his seat belt as Elisabeth jammed forward, then turned onto the highway.

It was a few miles before he was able to relax against the seat. They had done it.

But now there was no going back to his family for help. Tomas knew with certainty that Liam and Elisabeth had Joslyn.

And he wouldn't stop, wouldn't hesitate to hurt people, until he had her.

Elisabeth was a few miles from Penny Bay before she said, "Where are we going?"

"We can't take Joslyn back to Sonoma," Liam said.

Joslyn shook her head. "Tomas knows I'm with you."

"So we should find somewhere she can stay and be safe," Liam said.

"We can't leave her alone," Elisabeth argued.

"No, we won't do that. But I think I know someone who can help us. Head to Mendocino."

The farther they got from Penny Bay, the more Elisabeth felt like her lungs were opening up and she could breathe freely. She could feel Joslyn, sitting next to her, slowly stop trembling.

Elisabeth squeezed her hand. "You're all right now. We'll keep you safe."

Joslyn squeezed her hand back. "It's been a nightmare." Her head bent forward, and her straight dark hair fell forward over her face.

Joslyn closed her eyes and her jaw worked. "I'm so ashamed of what I've done."

"We know about the Tumibays and the shipping container," Elisabeth said gently. "You didn't have any choice."

"I shouldn't have gotten involved with Tomas in the first place." Her brow winkled in distress. "I was working at Perkins Electronics, putting myself through school, and he just came up and started flirting with me. I was floored he even noticed me. I was always the shy one at school. He was handsome, masculine, and he was so persistent."

Elisabeth remembered the charisma of her ex-boyfriend, how starstruck she'd been when they'd first started going out.

"It didn't take long to realize I'd made a mistake going out with him. I was going to find a way to leave him," Joslyn said softly. "I was working up the courage when he... My dad..." Tears began to flow down her cheeks. "It was my fault. If I hadn't been dating Tomas, Dad might still be alive."

"Stop thinking like that," Elisabeth said fiercely. "You're not to blame for the crimes Tomas committed."

Joslyn sucked in a deep breath, which calmed her. "You're right. It's what Hannah told me, too."

"Who's Hannah?"

"She's the woman who I was working for in Oregon." Joslyn gave a watery smile. "She's been wonderful. She was there for me when I lost..." Her face abruptly fell.

Dread began to pool in Elisabeth stomach. They'd suspected Joslyn was pregnant. "Did you have a miscarriage? Oh, Joslyn." She squeezed her hand again.

Joslyn blinked away more tears. "The stress and fear took a toll on my body. I didn't expect it, but I really wanted my baby. Hannah helped me through it. She's been praying for me and teaching me about grace."

"Grace?" Elisabeth was confused.

"God's grace," Joslyn said. "About how Jesus died for me, and no matter what I've done, I'm forgiven. I didn't think it would be so comforting, but it's been helping me so much. I feel so much less alone."

Elisabeth had become used to feeling alone. She realized that she was tired of it, but she also wasn't sure if she was ready to believe in a God who allowed bad things to happen to His people. How could Joslyn find God comforting in the midst of all the things that had happened to her?

"I was almost happy," Joslyn said. "I don't know how Tomas found me."

"Did you go to a clinic?" Liam asked.

Joslyn nodded. "I had to use my real name, but they promised me that the medical records were secure."

"The Bagsics probably hired another skip tracer who hacked into servers, looking for mention of you. But how'd they find you in Penny Bay?"

"They must have found out I hitched a ride with that farmer," Joslyn said. "They'd only need to ask at the stores on the farmer's route to see if anyone saw me." She wrapped her arms around herself. "I have such a hard time believing that there's any way to get away from them."

"I have somewhere to hide you," Liam said. "I have a cousin with a house in the mountains around Mendocino. He works for the county sheriff's department, so he can both hide you and protect you."

"For how long?" Joslyn said. "I can't hide forever."

Elisabeth didn't want to ask this, but she had to. "When Tomas killed your father, did you see it?"

She swallowed and nodded. "I was hiding in the kitchen cupboard. I thought for sure he'd find me. But Dad told them he didn't know where I was, and then they…" She cried softly for a few minutes.

"We will put him away," Elisabeth said. "We won't let him get away with that."

"But you don't understand," Joslyn said. "I can't testify

about the murder. Other people who testified against the Bagsics disappeared...."

"I saw something else that might help the case," Liam said.

Elisabeth peered at him. "You did?"

"I saw a Bagsic member in Penny Bay who was wearing Felix's vintage Rolex watch."

"Who was it? What was he wearing?" Joslyn asked.

"Purple silk shirt, black slacks, gray tie. He had a computer."

"That's probably Richard Mendoza. He does a lot of Tomas's computer work. He was there with Tomas in Dad's apartment that night."

"What I wouldn't give to get my hands on his computer," Elisabeth murmured.

"You can also testify about what you overheard Tomas say about the shipping container," Liam said to Joslyn.

Joslyn shuddered. "What about the Tumibays? Daniel was the only one I saw, but I told him about the shipping container. He'll need to keep me quiet about the fact I told him."

"We found the shipping container on Tumibay property," Elisabeth said. "I gave all the information to my contacts at the FBI. They're tracing it now."

"We will not stop investigating until it's safe for you to come out of hiding." Liam had a quietness and confidence that visibly calmed Joslyn. She nodded.

They switched off driving when they stopped for gas, and Liam drove to his cousin's house deep in the mountains, a little ways off the winding road into Mendocino. The house was newly built, two stories with lots of long windows, surrounded by redwood trees. Elisabeth imagined that the owner could feel as though he was living in the middle of the forest glade rather than within the walls of a house.

Liam had called ahead, and Jeremy came out of the house to meet them as the pickup truck drove up the gravel driveway. He was tall and lean, similar in build to Liam, and he moved with the fluidity and grace of an athlete.

As Liam and Jeremy talked, Elisabeth hugged Joslyn goodbye. "I'll call you to check up on you and keep you updated."

"Don't worry too much about me." Joslyn looked up at the starry sky, framed by the tops of the redwood trees high above. "I can't think of a more beautiful place to hide out. Although I'm dying for a Starbucks coffee."

Elisabeth smiled.

"I'll be praying," Joslyn said. "I have to believe that God will save me—will save all of us somehow."

The thought of being able to release her burdens suddenly seemed amazing to Elisabeth—and too good to be true. She was starting to realize just how tired she was. Maybe…maybe there was something there….

Or maybe there wasn't. Maybe this Christianity thing was only for people who had family members who loved them.

Maybe she was fooling herself into thinking she wasn't meant to be alone.

They drove out of Mendocino, Elisabeth at the wheel, and she was still lost in her thoughts when Liam got a call on his cell phone. "Hey, Shaun.…What?"

She turned at the sharpness of his voice. Had something happened to his family?

"Do you trust him?" Liam said into his phone. "Okay, we'll call him."

"What is it?"

"A Bagsic member called Shaun with a message for you." Liam's tone was wary, but there was curiosity in his voice, too. "He says he's willing to give us evidence against Tomas."

SIXTEEN

It had to be a trap. Liam couldn't think it was anything less.

But what if it wasn't? Evidence against Tomas— With that, he could ensure Elisabeth's safety, and the safety of his family and Joslyn.

Elisabeth's expression was fierce. "Why would he be willing to do that?"

"We'll have to call him to find out."

Shaun had said that the Bagsic member had called his workplace at the Joy Luck Life Hotel and Spa and left the message to pass to Liam. He'd given a phone number, which Shaun texted to Liam.

He put the phone on speaker, and a man answered after only one ring. "Yeah?" A high male voice.

"This is Elisabeth," she said.

"You called." The man heaved a sigh. "I wasn't sure if you would."

"What do you want?" Liam said.

"You guys are skip tracers, right? You can help me disappear? I'll give you evidence against Tomas if you can help me." The man spoke rapidly, nervously.

"Why are you doing this?"

"I don't want to do this anymore and there's no other way out of the gang except in a body bag."

He seemed sincere. Was Liam being too trusting? Did

he want to believe the man because he seemed to have the answer to his problems? "What kind of evidence?"

"A flash drive. I lifted the info from Richard Mendoza's computer."

The Bagsic in the internet café with Felix's watch. "We'll meet and you can give it to me."

"I'll give it to Elisabeth." The man's voice grew stubborn. "She helped Joslyn. She's a straight shooter."

"You're not meeting her alone," Liam snapped. He wasn't sure if the look Elisabeth gave him was grateful or surprised at his protectiveness, but at least she didn't look offended.

The man hesitated, then said sulkily, "Fine. You can tag along. But no cops."

Liam didn't respond to his demand about police. "Where are you?"

"I'm hiding off Tyndall Road."

That was near Liam's shabby duplex. That might work. "Meet us here in two hours." He gave his address.

"Two hours?" the man whined. "Don't be late."

"What's your name?" Elisabeth asked.

"You don't need it." And he hung up.

Liam and Elisabeth looked at each other for a long moment. "Do you think this is wise?" Elisabeth asked.

"I think it's worth a shot. I'll call Detective Carter about having policemen there."

"Where is this place?"

"It's my home—a duplex outside of Sonoma, surrounded by vineyards. The other buildings by me are vacant and my duplex neighbor, Mr. Brummell, is away for the holidays. No one around who could get hurt, but plenty of places for policemen to hide in the vineyard rows."

"That's a good plan."

Liam checked his watch. It had taken them four hours to get from Penny Bay to Mendocino, and it would take another couple hours to get back to Sonoma. "If Tomas

left Penny Bay the same time we did, he'll get back to Sonoma only a little before we will."

"Will it make a difference when we meet this guy?"

"I hope not." He called Detective Carter and told him
about the meeting. He also told him about Joslyn coming
forward to testify against Tomas for her father's murder,
and about the vintage Rolex watch Richard Mendoza was
wearing.

"I'll organize some officers to be at your place," the
detective said. "I'll make sure they're hidden."

Next, they called Joslyn, but she couldn't even say
for sure who the man on the phone could be—much less
whether or not he could be trusted. "He might be legit,"
Joslyn said. "But I don't remember any gang members with
a high voice."

The two hours back to Sonoma seemed to take forever.
What if the flash drive had no useful information? What
would be their next move? They were still waiting to learn
what the FBI had found out about the shipping container
and the Tumibay truck that was to have transported it.

He glanced at Elisabeth beside him. No matter what,
he'd make sure she was safe. He'd do everything he could
to ensure this meeting didn't go sideways.

It was after midnight when Liam turned into his driveway,
lined with hedges on one side and the duplexes on the other.
Beyond both were acres of grapevines, but the lack of street-
lights and house lights made the duplexes seem to swim in an
ocean of darkness. He parked in front of his house, the third
one, and the only one with the porch light burning fitfully.

"I don't see anyone here," Elisabeth said.

"He might be late." But he'd been hiding nearby hours
ago. Had he fallen asleep? "Let's go inside. It's cold."

He fitted his key into the lock and pushed the door open.
He heard a faint click.

Before his brain even coherently registered what was

happening, he'd thrown himself backward, propelling Elisabeth behind him. They landed on the ground and he covered her with his body.

An explosion ripped apart the night.

He knew it was happening even as the images flashed in front of him. The explosion reverberated in his brain, rattling his thoughts. His heartbeat galloped in his chest, and he was gasping, fighting to breathe as his friends died around him. He was going to die, and he'd never been so frightened in his life. The gunpowder burned his nose, and he tasted grit in his mouth.

"Liam."

He heard Elisabeth's voice and clung to it like a man dangling from a ledge. She pulled him from the nightmare. She was softness and sanity in the midst of desolation.

His head was in her lap. The flames from his house made her flicker from orange to yellow to darkness. He was in Sonoma. He was with Elisabeth.

And suddenly he began to sob.

The pain bubbled up from deep inside him. His chest was tight, his muscles knotted. He wrapped his arms around her and felt her hands on his head, his shoulders, rubbing his back.

He just wanted the pain to stop. He wanted it all to stop. He just wanted to be whole again. He was so tired. He was so lost.

"Are you all right? We have to get you away from the flames."

There were men around them, illuminated by the fire. The policemen who had been hiding in the vineyard.

"Liam, come on." She lifted his head from her lap, and then she was helping him stumble away from the house. They crossed the hedge and sat on the edge of the dirt lane. She put her arms back around him and leaned him against her. He breathed in her scent of oranges and flowers.

He didn't know how long they sat there. He heard the policemen calling the fire truck, making sure the other houses were empty. At one point he thought Detective Carter might have come up to him and laid a gentle hand on his shoulder, but the policeman didn't say anything; he just disappeared back into the darkness.

"Liam," Elisabeth said softly.

"I'm okay now."

"No, Liam. You're not." There was a firmness and authority in her voice, and yet she was still gentle. "I've worked extensively with abused women. When they are at the end of their strength, they have to reach out for professional help."

"I went to counseling. It didn't help, so I stopped."

"You need to go back." Her hand stroked his head, caressed his cheek. "And you need to talk to your family about what you're going through."

"I can't burden them with this. First my dad's leukemia, then the two gangs. I just can't put even more on them."

"Liam, they can support you through counseling. They can just be there for you. They can…" She swallowed. "They can pray for you."

When was the last time he'd asked them to pray for him? For something important, not just that he'd find his lost keys or that his beat-up truck would start? He was embarrassed to admit that he couldn't remember. He hadn't shared any of his problems with them. He hadn't wanted to worry them. He'd wanted to solve this on his own.

Look how well that had turned out.

He realized that the problem was that he'd been trying to do everything in his own strength.

Cast all your anxiety on Him because He cares for you.

"Liam, promise me you'll go back to counseling." Her fingertips smoothed over his brow.

He took a deep breath. "I promise."

"And promise me you'll talk to your family."

He didn't answer her. He remained leaning against her, listening to her breathing.

"Liam."

"I promise."

She squeezed his shoulders. He felt her cheek against his head.

"Liam, Elisabeth, the paramedics are here." It was Detective Carter. "I want them to look at both of you."

Liam slowly got to his feet, finally realizing the flames were out. There was some scorching around his doorway, but the damage looked minimal.

"This way, miss." A female paramedic led Elisabeth away first. She looked familiar. Maybe she'd been at one of their earlier confrontations.

"How are you doing, son?" Detective Carter's gravelly voice was kind.

"I'm fine, sir."

The detective simply nodded slowly. He reached into his jacket and pulled out a slim card case. He handed Liam a white card, then walked away.

It was the business card for a counselor. Liam tucked it into his pocket.

He stared at his house, and now realized he smelled gasoline. Maybe that was what had caused him to react so quickly when he'd opened the door.

But why would the Bagsics try to kill them? They knew Liam and Elisabeth knew where Joslyn was—killing them wouldn't do anything to reveal her location. Didn't they still want her?

Officer Joseph Fong came to take his statement. Liam asked him, "No one was hurt?"

"Aside from you two? Not really, just a few burns on the firemen. The fireman I talked to said it looked like the bomb was way at the back of the house, although it was triggered by the front door."

Why wouldn't the Bagsics have put the bomb near the front door? Wouldn't that have given it maximum effect? And *was* it the Bagsics, or the Tumibays, who'd planted the bomb? Liam leaned more toward the Bagsics. In most of their dealings with him, they'd been calculated and organized.

And suddenly he knew where he'd seen that female EMT before.

"Where's Elisabeth?" Liam shoved past Officer Fong toward the ambulance. He grabbed the male EMT who had just come out of the vehicle.

"There you are," the EMT said, but Liam interrupted him.

"Where's the woman who was with you?"

"Woman? That's my partner." He nodded to another man who was treating a fireman sporting a burn on his forearm.

Panic gripped Liam by the throat. He tried to shout, but his voice came out reedy. "Where's the detective?"

"What is it, son?" Detective Carter appeared, his face serious.

"Elisabeth," he gasped. "Patricia took Elisabeth. The Bagsics have her."

Elisabeth awoke suddenly, covered in cold water that smelled like mold.

Tomas's evil face leered in front of her face. "Good morning, princess."

She jerked away from him, and ropes bit into her hands, tied behind her back. She sat in a heavy wooden chair with her ankles bound, also.

Tomas laughed and threw aside a bucket, which had apparently been filled with the foul water he'd tossed on her.

"Took her long enough to wake up." The high male voice came from her right. A young man in a gray T-shirt and wearing bright purple basketball shoes lounged against a table. He'd been the voice on the phone.

"Nice performance on the phone," she said.

The man preened. "I know. I missed my calling."

Sitting at the table but not even bothering to look at her was a man matching Liam's description of Richard Mendoza, typing on a laptop.

"Eyes front, princess." Tomas grabbed her chin and forced her to look at him. "Where's Joslyn?"

She said nothing, simply gave him a neutral look.

Tomas sighed, straightened and then backhanded her across her face.

The blow made her eyeballs feel like they were rattling around in her skull. Stars bloomed in her vision. She found herself going completely still, just as she used to when Cruise beat her. When she went quiet and limp, somehow the strikes had seemed to hurt less.

"I know you don't want to ruin that pretty face," Cruise/Tomas said. "Just tell me what I want to know and I'll let you go. Scout's honor."

"You were never a Boy Scout," she guessed.

It earned her another blow.

"You're a tough chick. I respect that. But, princess, there are three of us. When I get tired, I'll just get one of my friends to take over for me."

"Not me," Richard said, still typing on his laptop.

"I'll take double duty," said the younger man.

She tasted blood in her mouth. Not a lot yet. It would get worse. And this time, she wouldn't be able to just wait out Cruise's temper tantrum. They would continue until she told them, or until she died.

She didn't want to die. And yet she didn't want to give herself false hope that Liam or the police would be able to find her. She didn't even know where she was aside from the fact the room was cluttered like a large storage closet.

Then she heard Monica's voice.

Even in the midst of suffering and pain and loneliness, He's there with us. He loves us, and we're not alone.

No, that wasn't true. She was all alone with these men, and they would hurt her even worse than Cruise ever had.

Joslyn's voice cut through her mind.

I have to believe that God will save me—will save all of us somehow.

Oh, God, she prayed.

Why would God answer her? She'd been thumbing her nose at Him for so long. He couldn't truly care about someone like her, someone who wouldn't believe in Him.

But God had saved Liam. He'd caused her to overhear him being attacked over her cell phone. Liam wasn't perfect, but God was his best bud.

Would God want to be her best bud?

Oh, God, please save me.

The tears began to fall down her cheeks, off her chin. She was so scared.

God, please take care of me.

And then somehow, in a way she couldn't even begin to describe, she knew she wasn't alone.

She closed her eyes. Dug deep. And believed.

When she opened her eyes, she looked straight at Tomas's arrogant face and said, "Bring it."

Shaun arrived at the duplex just as Liam was about to lose it. Detective Carter had been trying to get him to calm down and think clearly, and the EMT was threatening to sedate him.

Shaun took one look at Liam, then grabbed his shoulders in a hard grip, shoving his face right up to Liam's nose. "Chill. Now. Or I will punch you."

Liam jerked away from him. "Who needs enemies when I've got you?"

"That's the brother I know and love. Now take the time to explain what's going on."

Liam tried to be concise as he recounted what had happened, but he found himself stuttering and stumbling over words.

Elisabeth had been taken, right after he'd come to realize how he needed to trust in God more. It was like a sick and twisted test.

Was he really sincere in his faith? Could he rely on God's strength rather than trying to fix things himself?

He thought of all the things he'd never said to her. He might never get a chance to say them.

He could imagine her alone and helpless. In pain. Frightened. Despairing.

All he could do was let himself believe that the God who had parted the Red Sea, walked on water, moved as a pillar of fire, would not leave Elisabeth alone.

God, please help me find her.

"Okay, we need to find this Patricia." Detective Carter's voice was urgent and low. "What do we know about her?"

He thought back to the interview he'd had with her. Had she given Liam a business card? No.

"She seemed comfortable with her body," Liam said. "Like a dancer or a model. When she paid me, she'd emptied some things from her purse to reach the cash at the bottom—wads of receipts from Donny's."

"It's a chain restaurant," Shaun said. "There are dozens in California."

"It's a start," Detective Carter said. "What else?"

Then he realized, "Joslyn might know."

Liam called his cousin. The phone rang three times before he answered, since it was already past one in the morning, but then Jeremy quickly put Joslyn on the phone.

Liam gave a quick recap of the situation, then said,

"Joslyn, tell me if you recognize this woman." He described Patricia as best as he could.

"It sounds like Lauren, Tomas's cousin," Joslyn said.

His heartbeat picked up. "What's her last name?"

"Ramos. She lives in Napa."

"Thanks."

"Liam, please find her," Joslyn pleaded, and then hung up.

Detective Carter wasn't as excited as Liam expected him to be. "I'll call the Napa police department. Their new captain is a bit snippy about jurisdiction."

"Meaning?"

"Meaning, the Napa police will search Lauren's house, but they won't want Sonoma P.D. interfering. They might even get annoyed if I'm there, especially since I'll be waking the captain up." The detective went to phone the Napa police captain.

"So, what? We just wait here twiddling our thumbs?" Liam said to no one in particular.

"Hey." Shaun poked Liam's shoulder. "You're a skip tracer. So find her."

Shaun was right. What was he doing whining? He'd been trained for this.

"I need internet access," Liam said. He remembered Elisabeth's gentle voice, telling him to ask for help from his family. "Let's stop off at Dad's house and get Brady."

"Good idea. Nathan's there, too."

At the house, the four of them huddled around the kitchen table while Liam connected to the internet. The faces of the men were grave, but calm. At that moment, Liam was proud to be their brother and friend. They wouldn't fail him.

"There's only one Donny's in Napa," Liam said. "But I'm not sure how that'll help us."

"It's better than waiting around doing nothing." Shaun rose to his feet. "Let's go."

Liam phoned Detective Carter as they drove to Napa, telling him what he'd discovered.

"Liam, all I ask is that you don't interfere with police business."

"We're only driving around a few city blocks. Besides, our only lead is a bunch of receipts. But please tell the Napa P.D. where we are."

Most of downtown Napa was beautiful, a bit upscale—the perfect tourist destination. But the area where Donny's was located was on the very edge of the town, in a neighborhood a bit more run-down than other streets.

"There's the Donny's." Shaun pointed out the bright yellow sign.

"It's the only place open," Brady said. They passed a closed Mexican restaurant and a wine store.

"Didn't you say she looked like a dancer?" Nathan pointed ahead to a sign to their left that said Ellie's Gentleman's Club.

"They wouldn't take Elisabeth through the front," Nathan said. "Shaun, see if you can drive the car around the back."

He parked a street over and the four men walked the quiet sidewalk. Ellie's Gentleman's Club rose three stories above them, and music could be heard pulsing from within the square brick building. The back door was a heavy painted metal affair, and it was locked from the inside.

"I don't know if we could get in through the front door," Brady said. "They'll recognize Liam."

"They won't recognize me," Nathan said.

"You're not going in alone," Liam said.

"Of course he's not." Shaun clapped a hand on his friend's shoulder. "Hang tight. We'll head to the back and open the door for you."

Liam and Brady prowled around the back of the building. The windows were dark, boarded up. Slits of light filtered out from one, but it was high up and they couldn't see in.

"I'll look for something to stand on." Brady went around the corner to where they'd seen a Dumpster.

Liam stayed and looked up at the window. It was at least a foot above his head.

Wait a minute. Windows that high on the first floor meant that there must be a basement or sublevel underneath.

Liam crouched as he searched the base of the building. He saw some small windows, but they were also dark. He was turning the corner, heading toward Brady, when he caught sight of it—a small window set close to the ground, boarded up like the other one, with slits of light glowing feebly in the darkness of the alley between the two buildings.

"Brady," Liam hissed.

His brother joined him, kneeling by the window. "Can you see inside?"

Liam got on his stomach, feeling something slimy under his shoulder, and got his face close to the window.

Through the cracks, he could see inside a small room that looked like it was used for storage. At his angle, he only saw a set of metal shelves filled with toilet paper and bleach. He scooted sideways on the ground to get a different perspective.

And then he saw Elisabeth.

She was tied to a chair, and he only saw her in profile, but blood smeared her mouth.

"Brady, call Detective Carter. I see her!" Liam shifted sideways again to see more of the room, and that was when he saw Tomas.

He was livid, his face turning a maroon-purple color. "That's it!" he said, his voice muffled by the wooden boards and the thick glass window.

And then he pointed his gun straight at Elisabeth's head.

Time slowed down for Liam. His vision sharpened. He noticed the curve of her cheek, the scarlet of the blood.

Liam bolted to his feet and raced to the back door of the club just as it swung open.

"I feel like I need to burn my eyes out of their sockets," Shaun was saying, but Liam shoved him aside as he raced inside.

The hallway he entered was dark and low, and he almost tripped when he ran into the short flight of stairs at the end of it. Wrong staircase—he needed to go down, not up. He whirled, reaching for the flashlight in his pocket, but Nathan had one out already, and the light passed over a door set against the wall.

Liam threw himself against the door. It wasn't dead bolted, but the doorknob lock held. He threw himself against it again, grunting in his desperation, and this time, one of his brothers added his force to the door, and it burst open with a crash.

He leaped down a short flight of stairs, directly into a large man who had been standing near the bottom. They went down in a tangle, and Liam swung an elbow at the man's head.

"I've got him!" Shaun said.

Liam jumped to his feet and dashed across the room. Straight for Tomas.

Something huge crashed sideways into him, and he went flying into a steel shelving unit. There had been a gang member there that he hadn't seen. He didn't wait to get his feet under him, but snapped up with a knee, then followed with blows to the man's head, shoulders, torso. They rolled, and then he grabbed the man's head and slammed it against the edge of a lower shelf of the shelving unit.

He saw Tomas raise his gun at him. While he'd been fighting the Bagsic, Tomas hadn't had a clear angle to shoot, but now he stared down at Liam with enraged eyes.

But Tomas had forgotten about Elisabeth. Apparently only her wrists and ankles had been tied, and she'd used the distraction to stand up from the chair and then get her arms in front of her. With a yell, she jumped and threw herself on Tomas's back, hooking her arms around his neck. Her momentum swung her sideways in an arc, and the two of them went down together.

Tomas elbowed Elisabeth in the gut. She curled up with an "Oof!" and Tomas untangled her arms from around his neck.

Liam fell on him. They rolled, knocking into more shelving units and dropping boxes of paper towels onto them. Then Liam got slightly behind Tomas and sliced his arm across the man's neck in a choke hold. He secured his hand against his other forearm and squeezed.

Tomas's legs kicked out. He twisted and jerked to try to break Liam's hold. From where he lay on the ground with Tomas, Liam could see Brady deliver a punch to the gang member he'd been fighting earlier, and the man crumpled to the ground.

In four minutes, Tomas was unconscious. Liam shoved his body away from him, then looked around for Elisabeth.

She flew at him, hooking her tied wrists around his neck, and then his mouth was on hers. Holding her close to him, he was aware of how precious she felt in his arms. And that he had almost lost her.

They came up for air, and then they both murmured at the same time, "I love you."

She smiled at him, brighter than sunlight, her eyes shining like dark gold. Her scent wrapped around him, orange and tuberoses.

"I never want to be afraid of losing you again," he said, his voice hoarse.

"Me, too." And then she kissed him again.

SEVENTEEN

Christmas with the O'Neills was loud, crowded, filled with food…and wonderful.

Elisabeth helped Monica clear away the ham and turkey leftovers from the dinner table. Patrick O'Neill lingered at the table, chatting with Detective Carter. She hadn't known until tonight that Monica's aunt Becca was dating Detective Carter. It was strange to see him in a nonofficial mood, especially when he told her to call him Horatio.

"So the four of those boys took out five Bagsic members?" Patrick said.

Horatio nodded. "There wasn't much left for the Napa police to do."

"If I'd been there, I'd have taken them all out in half the time." He laughed.

Brady was near the kitchen door holding his son, who looked almost as sleepy as his father after the huge meal, and talking with Liam.

"Tonight, maybe I can finally whip your tail on 'League of Legends.'" Brady grinned at him.

"Forget video games. Let's go for paintball. When's the last time you went?"

Brady groaned. "When you hit me on the neck and gave me a welt the size of Texas."

Liam smiled. "You're the one who exposed your jugular."

Brady looked fondly at his sleepy son. "Wait till this boy grows up. He'll vindicate his old man by destroying his uncle at paintball."

Monica's sister, Rachel, was washing dishes at the sink. "Elisabeth, you never finished telling me what happened with the FBI investigation into the Bagsics. You told me Tomas gave up his bosses?"

"He'd been working so hard to find Joslyn because the heads of the gang had threatened to kill him if he didn't do something to make up for the lost ephedrine shipment," Elisabeth explained as she found a plastic bag for the ham leftovers. "He had nothing to lose by giving them up."

"Did the FBI find their supplier in the Philippines?"

"They haven't told me, but I wouldn't be surprised if they've put something in motion. And they did search traffic cameras to find the truck the Tumibays used to move the shipping container, and got the license plate. They found it was hired by IRF Norris. They'll probably shut the company down, although first they're going to try to prove the connection to the Tumibays."

"That's going to cripple the Tumibays' money laundering," said Jane, Monica and Rachel's cousin, who was drying dishes. "Did you hear about the bodies they found?"

"What bodies?" Monica turned to her.

"Two Tumibay gang members," Jane said. "It was in the news."

"Were they the ones who had attacked you?" Rachel asked Elisabeth.

"One of them was—Lamar Garcia, the man with the fishhook scar on his face."

"I remember you mentioned him," Rachel said.

"The other one was Daniel, Faye's boyfriend, the one who had hurt Joslyn." Liam hadn't been as pleased about the two dead men. There was now no connection between Joslyn or Liam and the Tumibays, but the way it had ended—with the murder of two gang members—didn't sit right with him. But Elisabeth had to admit that it was a relief that with the Bagsics' troubles, the Tumibays were now lying low.

"How are they?" Rachel asked.

"Faye's with her mom, but she'll be able to go back to her life in San Francisco now that the threat against her is gone. Joslyn's with family in Los Angeles, but we invited her to move here to Sonoma in the new year."

"Really?" Jane's eyes glowed. "She and I had so much fun talking computers."

"Liam and I are seriously talking about going into business together," Elisabeth said. "Skip tracing, helping people stay safe." Protecting people, just as God had protected her and Liam.

"Joslyn would make a great skip tracer," Jane said. "Her computer skills are almost as good as mine."

"Oh-ho, modest much?" Monica teased her.

Suddenly there were warm arms that came up from behind her and wrapped around her stomach. Liam's voice tickled her ear, making her smile. "I came up with another name."

The two of them moved a little away from the giggling women. "Please tell me it's not something weird again like Macho Libre Skip Tracing Agency." She grinned at his face, inches away from her own.

"How about the Haven Agency? We can help people find their true—"

"Home."

His arms tightened around her.

She had found her home, in the love of God that filled her heart and made her feel alive, made her feel she belonged. She was done with being alone.

And Liam's love was her anchor, the gift she was finally able to grasp with both hands.

His mouth was inches from hers. "Sometimes I can hardly believe you're here with me."

She closed her eyes and kissed him.

She was home.

* * * * *

Dear Reader,

Thank you for joining me once again for this trip to Sonoma, California! In addition to my favorite small town, my hero and heroine traveled up and down the California coast, and I hope you enjoyed the adventure with them.

Penny Bay is loosely based off the quaint town of Mendocino in Northern California. It is one of my favorite places to visit because of the great restaurants, cozy wineries and beautiful forests and beaches.

When I wrote *Narrow Escape,* I knew that Liam O'Neill would eventually need his own story, and Elisabeth Aday showed up out of nowhere as the perfect woman for him. She is kind but tough, and only she has the ability to help heal him. I hope you've enjoyed watching them dodge bullets and fall in love.

You can find out more about my entire Sonoma romantic suspense series at my website, www.camytang.com.

I love to hear from readers! You can email me at camy@camytang.com or write to me at P.O. Box 23143, San Jose, CA 95123-3143. I post about knitting, my dog, knitting, tea, knitting, my husband's coffee fixation, occasional giveaways, food—oh, and did I mention my knitting obsession?—on my Facebook page: www.facebook.com/CamyTangAuthor. I hope to see you all there!

Camy Tang

Questions for Discussion

1. Liam was dealing with the traumatic memories of the incident in Afghanistan. Can you relate to his pain? What should his friends and family have done for him? What should he have done for himself?

2. Liam's family were strong Christians who were comfortable speaking about their faith. Can you relate to them or do you know someone like them? What is your own way of sharing your faith?

3. Elisabeth was upset at God because she couldn't understand why God would allow her father to abandon her and her boyfriend to abuse her. Have you been in a situation where you questioned why God allowed some evil to happen to you? How did you respond? How should we respond?

4. As things got worse, Liam just tried harder to protect Elisabeth on his own and gain some sense of control over the situation. Have you ever felt this way? How did you respond? What would you have done differently from Liam?

5. Liam had been trying to protect Elisabeth on his own strength, but he had to learn how to completely trust God instead. What does he learn about himself and his Heavenly Father? How does that impact the choices he makes at the end?

6. Elisabeth's theme verse is Isaiah 41:10 (NIV): "So do not fear, for I am with you; do not be dismayed, for

I am your God. I will strengthen you and help you; I will uphold you with my righteous right hand." What does that verse mean for you?

REQUEST YOUR FREE BOOKS!
2 FREE RIVETING INSPIRATIONAL NOVELS
PLUS 2 FREE MYSTERY GIFTS

Love Inspired®
SUSPENSE

YES! Please send me 2 FREE Love Inspired® Suspense novels and my 2 FREE
mystery gifts (gifts are worth about $10). After receiving them, if I don't wish to receive
any more books, I can return the shipping statement marked "cancel." If I don't cancel,
I will receive 4 brand-new novels every month and be billed just $4.74 per book in the
U.S. or $5.24 per book in Canada. That's a savings of at least 21% off the cover price.
It's quite a bargain! Shipping and handling is just 50¢ per book in the U.S. and 75¢ per
book in Canada.* I understand that accepting the 2 free books and gifts places me under
no obligation to buy anything. I can always return a shipment and cancel at any time.
Even if I never buy another book, the two free books and gifts are mine to keep forever.

123/323 IDN F5AC

Name	(PLEASE PRINT)

Address		Apt. #

City	State/Prov.	Zip/Postal Code

Signature (if under 18, a parent or guardian must sign)

Mail to the **Harlequin® Reader Service**:
IN U.S.A.: P.O. Box 1867, Buffalo, NY 14240-1867
IN CANADA: P.O. Box 609, Fort Erie, Ontario L2A 5X3

**Are you a current subscriber to Love Inspired Suspense books
and want to receive the larger-print edition?
Call 1-800-873-8635 or visit www.ReaderService.com.**

* Terms and prices subject to change without notice. Prices do not include applicable
taxes. Sales tax applicable in N.Y. Canadian residents will be charged applicable taxes.
Offer not valid in Quebec. This offer is limited to one order per household. Not valid
for current subscribers to Love Inspired Suspense books. All orders subject to credit
approval. Credit or debit balances in a customer's account(s) may be offset by any other
outstanding balance owed by or to the customer. Please allow 4 to 6 weeks for delivery.
Offer available while quantities last.

Your Privacy—The Harlequin® Reader Service is committed to protecting your
privacy. Our Privacy Policy is available online at www.ReaderService.com or upon
request from the Harlequin Reader Service.
We make a portion of our mailing list available to reputable third parties that offer products
we believe may interest you. If you prefer that we not exchange your name with third
parties, or if you wish to clarify or modify your communication preferences, please visit
us at www.ReaderService.com/consumerschoice or write to us at Harlequin Reader
Service Preference Service, P.O. Box 9062, Buffalo, NY 14269. Include your complete
name and address.

LIS13R

SPECIAL EXCERPT FROM

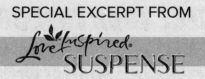

SWAT team member Isaac Morrison didn't plan to fall for his best friend's sister. But when Leah Nichols and her son are in trouble, he'll stop at nothing to keep them out of harm's way.

Read on for a sneak peek of
UNDER THE LAWMAN'S PROTECTION
by Laura Scott

"Stay down. I'm going to go make sure there isn't someone out there."

"Wait!" Leah cried as Isaac was about to open his car door. "Don't go. Stay here with us."

He was torn between two impossible choices. If someone had shot out the tires on purpose, he couldn't just wait for that person to come finish them off. Nor did he want to leave Leah and Ben here alone.

So far he wasn't doing the greatest job of keeping Hawk's sister and her son safe. If he'd been wearing his bulletproof gear he would be in better shape to go out to investigate.

Isaac peered out the window, trying to see if anyone was out there. Sitting here was making him crazy, so he decided doing something was better than nothing.

"I'm armed, Leah, so don't worry about me. I promise I'll do whatever it takes to keep you and Ben safe."

He could tell she wanted to protest, but she bit her lip and nodded. She pulled her son out of his booster seat and tucked him next to her so that he was protected on either side. Then she curled her body around him. The fact that she would risk herself to protect Ben gave Isaac a funny feeling in the center of his chest.

Leah's actions were humbling. He hadn't been attracted to a woman in a long time, not since his wife had left him.

But this wasn't the time to ruminate over the past. Isaac's ex-wife and son were gone, and nothing in the world would bring them back. So Isaac would do the next best thing—protect Leah and Ben with his life if necessary.

Don't miss
UNDER THE LAWMAN'S PROTECTION
by Laura Scott,
available January 2015 wherever
Love Inspired® Suspense books and ebooks are sold.

LISEXP1214

Love Inspired

JUST CAN'T GET ENOUGH OF INSPIRATIONAL ROMANCE?

Join our social communities
and talk to us online!
You will have access to the latest
news on upcoming titles and special
promotions, but most important,
you can talk to other fans about your
favorite Love Inspired® reads.

 www.Facebook.com/LoveInspiredBooks

www.Twitter.com/LoveInspiredBks

Harlequin.com/Community

LISOCIAL